Amber-Eyed Man

Also by Dorothy Garlock in Large Print:

Annie Lash
Dream River
The Edge of Town
Forever, Victoria
Home Place
Lonesome River
Ribbon in the Sky
River of Tomorrow
Sins of Summer
Tenderness
Wild Sweet Wilderness
With Heart
With Hope
With Song
Yesteryear

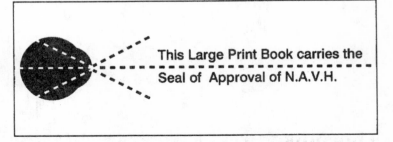

This Large Print Book carries the
Seal of Approval of N.A.V.H.

Amber-Eyed Man

Dorothy Garlock

Thorndike Press • Waterville, Maine

Published in 2006 by arrangement with Warner Books, Inc.

Thorndike Press® Large Print Famous Authors.

The tree indicium is a trademark of Thorndike Press.

The text of this Large Print edition is unabridged.
Other aspects of the book may vary from the original edition.

Set in 16 pt. Plantin by Christina S. Huff.

Printed in the United States on permanent paper.

Library of Congress Cataloging-in-Publication Data

Garlock, Dorothy.
    Amber-eyed man / by Dorothy Garlock.
       p. cm. — (Thorndike Press large print famous authors)
    Originally published under the name Johanna Phillips.
    ISBN 0-7862-8256-8 (lg. print : hc : alk. paper)
    1. Runaway wives — Fiction. 2. Mexico — Fiction.
  3. Large type books. I. Title. II. Thorndike Press large
print famous authors series.
  PS3557.A71645A82 2005
   813'.54—dc22   2005027645

To
Mary Bruza
— because she is my sister and
I love her.

As the Founder/CEO of NAVH, the only national health agency solely devoted to those who, although not totally blind, have an eye disease which could lead to serious visual impairment, I am pleased to recognize Thorndike Press* as one of the leading publishers in the large print field.

Founded in 1954 in San Francisco to prepare large print textbooks for partially seeing children, NAVH became the pioneer and standard setting agency in the preparation of large type.

Today, those publishers who meet our standards carry the prestigious "Seal of Approval" indicating high quality large print. We are delighted that Thorndike Press is one of the publishers whose titles meet these standards. We are also pleased to recognize the significant contribution Thorndike Press is making in this important and growing field.

Lorraine H. Marchi, L.H.D.
Founder/CEO
NAVH

* Thorndike Press encompasses the following imprints: Thorndike, Wheeler, Walker and Large Print Press.

Chapter One

A soft breeze caressed Meredith Moore as she gazed from the bedroom window out into the velvet dark of the Mexican night. Carrying with it exotic sounds and scents, it coolly bathed her face and gently lifted her pale, shoulder-length blond hair. She drew in her breath at the sight of the white fuscia and gardenia blossoms, glowing in the light of hanging lanterns, a border for the cobbled courtyard below. In the center, she could just make out a graceful mountain silhouetted against the darkening sky. As tired as she was from her journey, she could have looked out onto that scene forever, so different was it from everything she'd ever known. With an effort, she turned to finish unpacking the last of her suitcases.

Here again beauty greeted her. Softly lit by a pink-shaded lamp beside the bed, the room boasted deep rose bedcovers, matched by the drapes at the windows. When she moved toward the white dresser, painted with intricate gold designs on its curved front, her shoes sank deep into the soft white carpet. She soon found that the splendor of the bedroom was more than equaled by that of the attached bath. Eager to soak away the grime and fatigue of the long day, Meredith entered the turquoise and white room, and gasped with pleasure at the sight of the enormous tub, the glass-enclosed shower, the plush, fluffy bath towels hanging on gold bars and the bowls of tangy smelling salts and *potpourri* lining the marble top of the vanity.

After turning on the gleaming brass taps, Meredith scattered a cloud of bath crystals into the steaming cascade of water. As the haunting, seductive fragrance enveloped her, she settled gracefully into the tub, a smile on her generous lips. Perfect, she thought, just what the doctor ordered. Her immediate cares slipped away, and for the moment she could concentrate on relaxing — and could forget what had brought her to the secluded Mexican villa of Ward Sanderson, a man she did not even know.

The warm water of the bath lulled her, and Meredith forced herself to leave its comfort while she still had the energy to do so. She patted herself dry with a lamb-soft towel and returned to her room, her bare toes luxuriating in the rich carpet. Her hair, now a little damp, framed a heart-shaped face delicately and faintly sprinkled with freckles. An appealing face, with its straight nose, wide, generous mouth, and startlingly blue eyes, it seemed even more so now that her skin glowed like pale honey.

Lifting her hair with both hands, she piled it on top of her head and studied her reflection in the mirror. She didn't look one day older than twenty-five, though recently she'd felt at least one hundred. Meredith did notice, though, that wearing her hair up emphasized her slenderness and made her look younger. Abruptly she let the golden locks fall and turned to the bed to pick up her skirt and blouse.

Suddenly she leaped backward with a gasp. Something had pinched her bare toes, though her alarm came more from surprise than pain. But she was quickly put at ease when she looked down. Instead of the curling back of a venomous scorpion, a yellow-ribboned braid of dark hair peeked out from under the rose bedspread. She knew it could belong to none other than Maggie Sanderson, and she determined to wreak playful revenge on her host's four-year-old daughter.

Quickly, quietly, she walked to the other

side of the bed, then in a flash dived under it, reaching for the small wiggling figure. Despite her stealth and speed, however, Maggie escaped her grasp, and scrambled out to run screeching through the bathroom and into the bedroom beyond.

Meredith ran after her, her robe flapping around her bare legs. She arrived in the room in time to see two small feet disappear under the bed. She fell down on her knees and then flat on her stomach as she wiggled into the narrow space after the laughing, shrieking child. Grabbing the small sturdy body, she tickled her ribs and the child laughed even more, turning from side to side in an attempt to get away.

"So this is the monster that attacked my toe." Meredith nipped a small arm with her teeth. "I'll teach you, monster, to go around attacking people."

"No . . . No! I'm Princess Leia!" the child shouted between giggles.

"Oh, yeah? Well, I'm King Kong!"

The playful scene was soon shattered, however, when a voice boomed out, "What in the name of common sense is going on here?"

Meredith heard the deep voice before she saw the two shiny, black shoes planted firmly beside the bed. The child grew still at once, then a delighted, impish smile lit up her pixie face.

"Daddy!" In a flash she was out from under the bed.

Meredith could see the small, sandled feet beside the two large, black shoes. If ever in her life she wished the floor would open up and swallow her, this was the time. But, of course, no such miracle happened, and she attempted to climb out from under the bed with as much dignity as the circumstances allowed. She stood with her back to the man until she was sure the robe covered her, then turned her head up to look into the richest pools of amber she'd ever seen. She barely managed to stifle a gasp of surprise, but was unable to tear her eyes away from those brooding tawny depths, which despite her sudden appearance, bespoke a quality other than surprise. Was it hurt, Meredith wondered?

Yet while his eyes were soft, his voice was harsh as it broke the silence. "Who the devil are you?"

Meredith was frozen with shock. Her mouth opened and trembled. "Meredith Moore."

"Oh for God's sake!" he said in English before a torrent of Spanish curses fell from his lips. Stunned, Meredith watched his strange, light, tawny-colored eyes sweep over her. "Oh for God's sake!" he said again. "Jim didn't say. . . . I assumed you would be . . . well, to be frank, closer to retirement age!"

She licked her dry lips. "I have a ways to go, I'm afraid."

"I can see that!" He expelled a heavy breath, then lowered his gaze to Maggie, who had wrapped her arms tightly around his legs. He fondled the child's dark head before he returned his chilling gaze to Meredith, whose thin shoulders seem to brace themselves defensively. His eyes narrowed. "You're not at all what I expected," he said cruelly.

She took a quivering breath, despising the tears that sprang to her eyes.

"Daddy." Maggie shook his leg to get his attention. "I pinched her toe." Suppressing a giggle, she added, "She chased me."

His grim mouth relaxed as he looked down at the small face, but he seemed to grow tense as he turned his attention back to Meredith.

Though she had been desperate for a place to stay, Meredith had her pride. "I'm sorry I'm not what you expected," she said, trying not to lose herself in those eyes. "I'll leave at once." Bold words! She didn't know where she would go, but pride forced her to say them.

He didn't respond immediately, but allowed his gaze to flicker over her, the tawny eyes narrowed to mere slits. Then he gave a brusque gesture.

"We won't discuss it now. Be in the library in fifteen minutes."

For a long moment she didn't move. A play of emotions flashed through her — despair, doubt, and then resignation. She stared steadily at the man before turning toward her room, pride in every line of her slender figure and in the tilt of her poised head.

"Just a minute." His voice cut into the silence.

She stopped instantly. She turned, her face composed, but she knew her eyes shone unnaturally bright with tears between the fringe of her dark, gold-tipped lashes.

"Have you had dinner?" His voice was impersonal, crisp, and cool.

"No, I haven't." Her voice was equally cool.

Never removing his eyes from her, he nodded his head slightly and said, "Fifteen minutes."

"Certainly," she responded coldly. She managed to hold her head high as she left, but the more she walked, the more difficult it became to keep from sobbing out loud. As soon as she was far enough away from him, her pace quickened, and she ended up running into her room, already a haven, and flinging herself onto the comforting softness of the bed. Here she could sob until there was nothing left inside her.

She cursed her fate. Coming here had seemed like such a good idea! After having met the formidable Ward Sanderson, however, she wasn't sure. If only she hadn't seen Laura Jameson take her baby from the hospital that night, her life could have continued on its comfortable, safe way.

Though outwardly dramatic, the incident had at first seemed far from earth-shattering. Young and unmarried, Laura Jameson had been forced to give up her infant daughter for adoption. Yet she had wanted just a little time alone with her Jenny, and had seen nothing wrong with "borrowing" the child for a few hours. Meredith was touched by Laura's action, but became outraged when she learned that her own eyewitness testimony at an upcoming hearing could mean that the young woman might be forbidden from ever seeing her child again. Meredith could not help but remember her own childhood, a succession of drab holidays and forlorn birthdays, sometimes forgotten altogether by the foster family she happened to be with.

"How cruel!" Meredith had exclaimed to Jim Sanderson when the two commiserated about the turn of events over coffee a few days afterward. As the social worker on the case, Jim had been responsible for placing the infant with a young couple, the Thomases. Years ago, he had done the same for Meredith, bringing her from the orphanage to her first foster home, and ever since he had been a kindly uncle to her.

Jim nodded in agreement. "And the pity of it is," he said, "that I know Laura meant no harm by what she did. She just wanted to say goodbye. If only Bob Thomas had some time to cool off," he added glumly, "I'm convinced he'd change his mind about getting the court order." The two stared dismally into their coffee.

But only a few moments later, his eyes lit up. "Wait a minute!" he said, "I have a fabulous idea." He suggested that Meredith leave town for a few weeks so that she couldn't appear at the hearing. "My cousin Cullen lives in a magnificent home — an estate, really — in Guadalajara. I believe his brother Ward is there right now, along with his little child Maggie. I'm sure they wouldn't mind having a guest — especially for a good cause." Jim described his plan, his eyes dancing with pleasure and benevolent mischief.

"And I bet Ward would really welcome your company. I think you could be a big influence on Maggie — that feminine touch, you know."

"Why?" asked Meredith. "Has his marriage suffered the fate of so many nowadays? How did he get custody of the child?"

"As a matter of fact, he's never been married — the child was his younger sister's — Cullen's twin — but she was killed in the accident that paralyzed Cullen. Ward, of course, took the girl in as his own, and she's always been treated as his little girl. I'd be surprised if he hasn't spoiled her to death."

Meredith's blue eyes had widened in horror at hearing the tragedy that had struck the Sanderson family. How true it was, she mused, that even fantastic wealth could not shield anyone from pain. "I'm so glad Maggie had someone to take her in. . . ." Her voice trailed off as she remembered how lonely her own childhood had been.

Jim put his hand on hers. "Well just think how much better it'll be for both her and

Cullen to have you around. And how much it will help Laura Jameson."

Yet what had seemed like the perfect solution then seemed to be just a very bad mistake right now. If only she hadn't been so impulsive, Meredith thought as she dragged her exhausted body from the bed. In the bathroom mirror, her now puffy blue eyes stared dully back at her.

"No!" she said aloud, pulling herself up to her full height. She splashed her face with cool water, then patted it softly with one of the luxurious towels. "You will *not* let that man destroy you. You've worked too hard to be where you are."

As she applied her make-up, she fought to forget Paul, charming Paul — so handsome he was almost beautiful, and so subtly elegant and smooth that it took Meredith almost four years to realize that under the glossy surface there was absolutely nothing. She would never again allow a man, and especially not a handsome man, to do what Paul had done to her self-esteem. If this Ward Sanderson thought he could bully her, he had another think coming. After all, he was just a man. . . . Even though, for a time back in Maggie's room, she knew she could lose herself for all time in those tawny eyes.

Chapter Two

When Meredith emerged from her room fifteen minutes later, a young maid was waiting for her in the hall.

"O, Señorita," she exclaimed as she put out a hand to touch Meredith's rich turquoise blouse, *"Es muy bella!"* She then remembered her position, and quickly drew back her hand. Meredith could tell by the look in her velvet black eyes that the young woman feared a reprimand.

"Gracias," she replied quickly, employing almost all of her Spanish vocabulary. She smiled at the woman, and made a gesture toward a stunning silver and turquoise barrette in her raven hair. *"Muy bella,* also," she said, and they joined in laughter at Meredith's mixing the two languages.

Heartened by the success of the exchange, Meredith scoured her memory for just a little more of her high-school Spanish. *"Mi nombre . . .* Meredith," she said slowly.

The other woman laughed, and pointed a dainty hand toward herself. "Elena," she responded. Then, with a shy smile, she led Meredith downstairs to the lower corridor and indicated another door some distance along the hall.

"*Biblioteca, Señorita* Meredith," she said. "Li-bra-ree," she translated with a smile.

Meredith nodded, returned a very well pronounced, *"gracias,"* and continued down the hall to the room in which the man she had begun to think of as her tormentor waited. She pictured him pacing, lionlike, ready to devour her after one quick scrutiny with those tawny, jungle eyes. Then she caught herself up. Come on, Meredith, she scolded herself, if you keep thinking like that, you'll be back in the same boat you were in with Paul. Picking up her pace, she strode with determination toward what she now considered her "moment of truth."

Yet when she got close to the library, she hesitated. The door was slightly ajar, and her host was talking on the telephone. Unfortunately — or perhaps it was fortunate, she thought ruefully, since she now knew exactly where she stood — the connection was not a good one, and Ward Sanderson's deep voice boomed even more loudly than it would have normally.

"No, I'm not angry, Jim," he was saying, "but dammit, you should have told me a little more about her. You said a woman who'd been working at the Mayo Clinic. I assumed she was older. How the hell was I to know she looked like a college kid? Different? Ha! I'll bet she's different! How do you know?" During the silence, Meredith fumed. "I'll be the first to admit that Cullen needs young people around, but his mother will make things difficult once she hears about this. Norma's so damn afraid some girl will come along and catch Cullen's fancy that she can't keep her head on straight. Thank God she's away on another one of her cruises at the moment. Dammit, Jim! I know it's not a healthy situation, but what the hell can I do about it? Cullen's a grown man. He may not be able to walk, but there's nothing wrong with his head. This girl . . . doesn't she have any family you can send her to?" Silence. "Yes, I know that. I didn't say she was an opportunist because she was raised in foster homes. I said you should have . . ."

The awkwardness of the situation made Meredith clench her teeth. Fighting a strange tight feeling in her throat, she took a deep breath to build up courage before she faced the ordeal she knew was coming. The man stopped speaking, and she heard the click of the receiver being replaced. She waited a moment longer, then knocked on the door. When his command to enter came, it was with reluctance that she pushed open the door and entered the book-lined room.

He was standing in the shadows at the far end, his dark head outlined against the light draperies. He didn't bother to move as she closed the door.

"Sit down, Miss Moore." It was an uncompromising order.

Meredith remained standing. Her eyes never left the figure standing in the shadows. She heard a swift intake of breath and realized it was her own.

Ward Sanderson surveyed her with unconcealed impatience. "Please . . . sit down."

Deciding her legs were not all that reliable at the moment, she sought a small, straight-backed chair. She seated herself, then faced him.

He walked to the large, leather-covered desk in the middle of the room, and seated himself on the corner, all the while keeping his gaze fixed on her. Despite her determination to handle the interview coolly, she colored under his intent scrutiny, and felt as she once had when called to the principal's office in school for sticking her bubble gum in the hair of a girl who had taunted her about being a welfare child.

Suddenly Meredith realized that he was waiting for her to speak first. She straightened her back stubbornly and decided to say nothing, but her eyes seemed to be drawn to his, and he held them with a probing stare before moving from her face to her hair, then down the full length of her body. Although his glance was cool, almost clinical, Meredith's body responded to his scrutiny with an almost sensual shudder. She was furious. The conceited prig! Who in the world did he think he was to subject her to such treatment? What did he know about her kind of life? He'd never had to eat cornbread and milk for supper or put cardboard in his shoes to keep his feet out of the snow!

When he spoke his voice was softer than she expected. "How old are you?"

"Twenty-five." She was so angry she could hardly speak.

"Twenty-five," he repeated, meditatively. He leaned back and took a slim cigar from a box on the desk and with his eyes still on her he lit it with a silver lighter before he spoke again. "You look about . . . eighteen."

Meredith's lips tightened. "My problem, not yours." She said the words tensely.

A smile almost reached the tawny eyes.

Unexpectedly he leaned forward and the smell of the expensive Havana cigar smoke invaded her nostrils.

"You're not what I expected. Jim said you were a technician working in Rochester, Minnesota at the Mayo Clinic. He neglected to mention that you were young and attractive so I assumed you were older. After all, that's quite a responsible job you have, and the Mayo Clinic —"

Meredith did not let him continue. "Well, I'm a responsible person," she said calmly, though she was furious inside. "I'm sorry Jim misled you. Naturally I won't impose on your hospitality." She couldn't keep the words from coming, but bit back and swallowed her desire to tell him what she thought of him.

He drew deeply on the cigar, his dark brows drawn closely together. She glanced at him from beneath her lashes and his expression seemed to be more serious than angry. He continued smoking without taking his eyes from her face and she felt herself becoming unnerved by his stare. She racked her brain for something to say. Damn, why didn't he say *something?* Abruptly she stood up, but her knees felt weak from hunger and the strain of the trip, and she held tightly to the back of the chair.

His lips barely moved, but she heard his words distinctly. "Sit down."

She did, wishing desperately she could leave this man's presence before she made some undignified outburst, just to relieve the tension. She sat on the edge of the chair, silent, a mingling of inquiry and rebellion on her face. The thought flashed through her mind that this was the kind of man Paul would like to be — rich, powerful, confident. But the shallow Paul would never make it! Sanderson would ooze confidence if he stood ragged and barefoot.

He continued to look at her. The tawny, wide-spaced, clear eyes were the color of a young lion. They were fascinating eyes, unwavering, and, as she had the first time she met him, Meredith sensed an undercurrent of pain just below their amber surface. Deep crinkly grooves marked the corners, put there when the eyes had squinted against the sun. There were other lines, too, that experience, tiredness, or bitterness had made.

But before she could speculate further, he stood suddenly, picked up some papers from the desk, and took them to a file cabinet at the end of the room. For the first time Meredith noticed he limped slightly when he walked. She also remarked upon the breadth of his shoulders and the narrowness of his hips in the dark business suit. He was, she was forced to admit, an impressive man, tall, lithe, with a head of crisp, springy brown hair, that blended well with his tanned skin.

She dreaded the moment when he would turn and look at her. This man had caused her confidence to come tumbling down. The golden glow of the few carefree minutes she had spent with his little girl diminished and died beneath the onslaught of his re-buff. She wished, desperately, that she could think of something cutting to say, to fling his hospitality in his face and leave!

He came toward her, but just walked past her to the door. With his hand on the knob he said, "Let's have dinner."

Meredith wasn't sure she had heard right. She got unsteadily to her feet and smoothed her skirt with shaky hands.

"Come on." He opened the door and stepped aside for her to pass through. Then he escorted her down the corridor and into a small room where a fire burned in a stone fireplace. A table was set for two and beside it stood a cart with gleaming dishes of food. He lifted the lid from a large tureen and a delicious aroma made her feel even hungrier than she had just moments before.

Meredith stood inside the door. "Sit here."
He held a chair out for her. His movements
were easy and flowing despite his limp.

He placed a large bowl of soup in front of
her, then served himself and sat down
across from her. Meredith was almost afraid
to lift her trembling hands to the bright sil-
verware. More than anything in the world
she wished to keep this man from knowing
how crushed she was, how miserable she
felt, how his attitude brought back memories of years spent, unwanted, in foster
homes. Not for anything would she reveal
her true feelings or anything at all about
herself to this stony-hearted man who was,
as far as she could tell, as compassionless
and self-centered as Paul.

He buttered a large, hard roll and placed
it on a dish beside her plate.

"These are called *bolillos* and are delicious with soup."

Meredith glanced at him quickly. Damn
him! Why was he acting now as if she were a
guest? He was eating and she was relieved
his eyes were on the food and not on her.
She began to eat, pleased that it was easier
than she thought it would be. She had been
sure she would be unable to swallow. Her
tension eased and she had finished half the
soup when he spoke again.

"While we're eating I'll tell you about Maggie."

His words were a shock, causing her to halt the spoon in midair. She said nothing, nor did she look at him, and he continued.

"Maggie has spent the last few weeks here with my brother. In a few more weeks I'm taking her home where she'll start public school. I don't suppose you know that I actually live in Tulsa, although of course I do spend a lot of time here looking after the family plant in Guadalajara. At any rate, because Maggie was born in the fall, she'd normally have to wait another year to go to school, but I was told she'd be taken if she could pass an exam. It's difficult to believe that there can be entrance requirements for kindergarten, but that's what they tell me, and I'm not at all certain Maggie will qualify. The school prepared a list of the things she should know and when Jim called and said you needed a place to lose yourself for a while, I assumed you would be willing to take on that chore."

"And now that you have seen that I'm not middle-aged and fat, you don't think I'll be able to handle it." It was a petulant thing for her to say and she knew it. The twinkle in his eyes told her he knew it too.

"Maggie has had a procession of people

looking after her. Despite all that, she's a well-adjusted little girl. What she really needs is children to play with. It's important for her to get into school now."

Meredith continued to spoon the soup into her mouth. He seemed to be determined to make conversation. "Jim said you took your training at Tulsa Memorial, but were in Rochester for the last few years. Did you like the work?"

She ignored his question, preferring to pose one of her own. "Now that you've seen the opportunist who was raised in foster homes at government expense, what do you think?" After speaking the words, Meredith carefully placed her spoon beside her plate and her eyes fastened on his face. When she looked at him she saw a glimmer of admiration cross his face, and his lips twitched slightly. He raised his brows.

"I eavesdropped," she said matter-of-factly.

He chose to ignore her confession. "Are you a good x-ray technician?" he asked again.

"I'm a very good technician." Her eyes held his. "I was top in my class or I wouldn't have received an offer to work at the Mayo Clinic."

"Have you had any experience with

paralytics?" He had stopped eating and was looking at her intently.

"Only when they were brought to my department for x-rays."

"Do you know about my brother?"

"Jim told me he lost the use of his legs — and you said he was smothered by his mother."

He smiled. It seemed to her that a curtain had been raised. "You don't miss much, do you?"

"I can't afford to. I'm all I've got."

Meredith wondered how long her courage would last. She had had the pleasure of telling him she knew of his small-minded suspicions of her, and she had let him know she wasn't frightened of him. At least a little of her pride had been salvaged.

He removed the empty soup bowls and replaced them with a plate containing a small steak. Meredith shook her head, knowing she couldn't possibly eat the meat. He resumed eating before he spoke. "Eat what you can. You look as if the wind could blow you away."

She felt a stab of resentment and her heart pounded in response to her anger. Who was he to tell her what she should or should not do? She could look after herself, thank you very much.

Seeing the anger in her face, he grinned, his even white teeth a contrast to his tanned cheeks. The effect was at once devilish and attractive, and reminded Meredith of her image of him, a voracious lion, ready to devour whatever — or whomever — he chose. He finished his steak without saying anything else. Meredith managed to swallow only a few bites.

Yet the butterscotch custard, warm and laced with heavy cream, was another matter. When she first tasted it, her eyes widened in appreciation. She caught Ward looking at her and deliberately refused to look away.

"It's called *flan* and is Carmen's specialty. Do you like it?"

"Very much," she murmured.

They finished the meal in silence, and when Ward rang a bell, Elena came and piled the dishes onto a serving cart and rolled it to the door. He spoke to her in Spanish. She flashed a quick smile in Meredith's direction, then nodded to Ward before going out of the room.

Meredith felt uncomfortable. She didn't know if she was dismissed, and would be damned before asking if the master of the house had finished with her. He, however, seemed totally at ease, and why not? He was in charge. He stood and moved to a table for a cigar. Meredith rose, too, intending to leave the room, but was stopped by a wave of his hand. He motioned her to a deep, brown leather chair and she knew her ordeal was not yet over.

Elena returned with a tray and placed it on a table beside her chair.

"I thought you might enjoy our Spanish chocolate."

Looking far more composed than she felt, she accepted the cup he handed her and murmured her thanks. He poured a cup for himself and, sitting down, surprised her by saying, "Tell me about yourself."

Meredith had no intention of being taken in by a few kind words.

"You know all there is to know, Mr. Sanderson," she replied with a shake of her head. "Jim thought we could avoid unnecessary suffering if I didn't testify at a court hearing back in Minnesota about a child-snatching, or rather child-borrowing, incident I witnessed. Naturally I could have disappeared somewhere in the States, but Jim was insistent that I come here. He said you could use someone to help take care of Maggie. Apparently he was wrong. If I could trouble you for transportation into Guadalajara tomorrow, I'll check into a hotel."

As soon as she'd said the bold words, she chastised herself. Damn! Her pride made her so reckless. What would she do if she couldn't use any of her credit cards here? But she didn't allow any of the apprehension she was feeling to show in her face, and she looked at him with wide, clear eyes.

"Are you always so confident?" he asked.

"No, not always," she answered honestly.

"I know what happened to you in the hospital. Jim filled me in on that. He finds your sympathy for the young mother admirable. You're lucky to have him for a friend, you know. But I want to know more about you. Your plans. Your ambitions."

She was silent for as long as it took her to fight down the angry words that leaped to her lips. What nerve! He sat there like the master inquisitor! Somehow she managed to swallow an angry retort. She must be prudent. In a foreign country with little money and no transportation, she simply wasn't in any position to take offense to his prying. But — dammit — she didn't have to bare her soul to him either. Resentment of his attitude showed in the look she gave him.

"Mr. Sanderson." Her voice was wooden with control. "I fail to see how you can possibly be interested in my personal ambitions. You seem to think I came here under false pretenses, but let me assure you I did not come here to ingratiate myself with you or your brother. I am not seeking a rich husband. That you find me unsuitable to be in your home is your privilege, but to pry into my personal life is not."

Inside her breast her heart was thudding like a sledgehammer at her own temerity. It was unreal that she could have spoken these words to this man. She was a guest in his home. An unwanted one, but a guest nevertheless. She closed her eyes for only a second and when she opened them he was still sitting there, his head resting against the back of the chair, his eyes locked onto hers. He looked deep, as if he were looking into her past, her present, and her future. His face was expressionless and his words when they came shocked her, for she had expected a cruel retaliation to her brashness.

"Does anyone call you Merry?" His voice was almost lazy as if he were talking to himself.

Surprised by the question, Meredith shook her head.

"Then I shall," he said softly. He sat up and flexed his shoulder muscles wearily. "It's been a long day. Go to bed, Meredith Moore. In the morning I'll dig out that list of requirements for Maggie."

Meredith's lips parted in dismay. "You want me to stay?"

He got to his feet and stood looking down at her, a somewhat puzzled expression on his leathery face. "Yes, Merry. I want you to stay."

She made an attempt to stand, then sank back down, a pulse throbbing noticeably in her throat. Color had seeped from her face and she felt light-hearted. Was he deliberately trying to confuse her? She pushed back a tendril of pale gold hair and stared at him.

A smile creased his cheeks, crinkled the corners of the tawny eyes and took away some of the strain from his tired face. He reached down a hand and pulled her to her feet. As he looked at her his incredible eyes softened and suddenly they seemed to envelop her in a warm snare of tender amusement. His hand came up and stroked her cheek. It was a large hand, strong but surprisingly gentle. Even his voice was deep and gentle as he chided her.

"Don't try to figure me out, Merry *mía*."

He turned her toward the door and in her confused state she was scarcely aware she was being conducted to the foot of the steps leading to the upper balcony. On the first step she turned, her face level with his, a curiously guarded look on her face.

He was standing very quietly, his eyes probing hers with a startling intensity. She hesitated, then started up the steps. Once she reached the top she looked back, but the hall was empty, and the last few minutes she'd spent with him seemed like a dream.

Chapter Three

The next morning Meredith was up, dressed, and standing beside the window when the sun made its first appearance. She had spent a restless night, her thoughts preoccupied by the people she had just met. Neither Paul, the clinic, nor Laura Jameson had entered her mind. Ward Sanderson was another story. He had floated in and out of her dreams all night long. She wasn't sure why, but even now it made her faintly uncomfortable to think about him.

She looked down into the courtyard where the sun was brilliant on the blue mosaic tiles that surrounded the fountain. Made of lapis lazuli and patterned as intricately as a Persian carpet, the tiles were laid the width of the courtyard. In the shady oasis of a poinsettia tree was an inviting bench. The peaceful scene should have given her pleasure, but it didn't. Whatever was wrong with her, she asked herself impatiently as she moved restlessly from the window.

On impulse she threw on a lavender

sundress and left her room. As she walked slowly down the carpeted stairs through the quiet house, it occurred to her that the dwelling boasted so many wings and court-yards that a large number of people could live there without intruding on one another. Still, was it large enough for her to avoid Ward Sanderson? She doubted it.

On reaching the courtyard, she was pleased to find that the sunlight was already warm. She faced the sun for a moment, her chin uplifted, eyes closed, and the palms of her hands extended. The warmth was deli-cious and seemed to penetrate deep inside, melting her worries away. Now, faint sounds of a child's voice came to her. She crossed the courtyard, and moved toward the back of the house. It seemed a long distance to Meredith until she realized the walkways branched off and came together, dividing plots of the garden. She rounded a corner and could see the glimmer of water in a swimming pool. She heard splashing and Maggie's excited voice.

"Don't let them see you, Merry."

Somehow Meredith wasn't startled by her host's voice. Ward stood in the shade of a flowering shrub. Wearing bathing trunks, he was rubbing his head with a large bath towel.

"Why not?" She surprised herself because the words came more easily than she expected.

"Cullen is teaching Maggie to swim. He'll be embarrassed if you see him getting out of the pool."

"Of course. I understand." Meredith nodded. She would be considered one of his peers. In the hospital, many young disabled men were reluctant to let young nurses assist them.

As if it were the most natural thing in the world, he took her hand. "Let's go back and give Cullen time to get out of the pool."

She was almost breathless. Why was his hand so rough and hard? Rich men were supposed to have soft, smooth hands. She had to walk quite close to him on the narrow path and she noticed his limp was more pronounced when he walked on the rough cobblestones. He was taller than she remembered. She had been able to look straight into Paul's eyes when they faced each other, but she only came up to this man's chin.

They stopped beneath a latticed portal. A jungle of flowering vines and other leafy greenery hung from the ceiling. The perfume from the plants was faint and sweet.

Ward released her hand and wrapped the large towel about his waist.

"Cullen is an excellent landscape engineer. He laid out these gardens and designed the fountain. Lately he's lost interest in everything except the plants in his rooms and his magic. I had to twist his arm to get him to teach Maggie to swim. I could have done it myself, but he and Maggie have a special relationship and I played on that."

"Doesn't his condition allow him to work?" Meredith looked up into tawny eyes and decided that she liked them — this morning, anyway. Last night they had been more ferocious.

"I suspect it has more to do with my stepmother. She's always been a possessive mother, and since the accident she's had an excuse to keep Cullen with her," Ward explained.

Suddenly Meredith felt annoyed at his cavalier attitude toward Cullen, just as she felt resentful at the strange hold he had begun to exert on her.

"Why do you allow it?" Her eyes challenged him.

"Allow what?" he countered brusquely.

Meredith was satisfied that he seemed annoyed by her bluntness. "Allow your stepmother to dominate your brother's life?"

"Why should I interfere? Cullen is a twenty-five-year-old man and if he doesn't have the backbone to tell his mother he can take care of himself, then he deserves to be henpecked!"

"You don't mean that," she replied calmly. "I can't believe you don't care enough about him to help him stand up to her."

He looked at her as if she had lost her mind. He stood quietly for a moment and when he spoke it was with puzzlement in his voice. "Do you always jump in with both feet?"

For an instant she was stumped for something to say, but she came up with a quick answer. "What have I got to lose?"

He laughed. She forgot herself and laughed with him.

"Do you want to take a swim?"

"No." Her answer was too abrupt so she softened it. "No, thank you."

"Afraid you'll ruin your hairdo?"

"What hairdo? It's just that I don't have a suit."

"That can be fixed."

"I don't swim."

He walked away from her and said over his shoulder, "I'll tell Carmen you'll breakfast with Maggie and me."

She watched him move away and wondered about his leg. Her medical knowledge told her that his was not a recent scar. The operation must have taken place years before, probably when he was a teenager.

Not knowing what to do with herself, she went back to her room and applied a touch of lipstick, then ran a comb through her hair.

When she went downstairs, it was with Maggie's hand tucked firmly in her own. The little girl was a delight. She had come into Meredith's room, wet braids hanging over her shoulders and an impish grin on her face, with Carmen, the cook, right behind her scolding in broken English.

"Hair not dry, little . . . mule!"

Together they had unbraided Maggie's hair and sat her under the big drier in the bathroom. Afterward Meredith had brushed and rebraided it while Maggie kept up an endless chatter. The child lived in an almost imaginary world, talking about her dolls and stuffed animals as if they were living creatures. Meredith almost felt sorry for her. She did need other children to play with.

Breakfast on a shaded terrace was easier than Meredith had thought it would be. Maggie acted as a buffer between her and

41

Ward. She watched him with his daughter. He didn't even remotely resemble the stern-faced man of last night; although more relaxed now, he was far from careless in his attitude toward the little girl. When she spoke he listened closely to what she was saying. And Maggie, Meredith was surprised to discover, took on a more mature personality when she was with him.

"How are the swimming lessons coming?" He had placed on her plate scrambled eggs from a covered tureen and was buttering a slice of toast.

"Unk said I paddle like a puppy." She giggled. "Unk said I can't use the doughnut to keep me up any more. He said I wouldn't learn to swim."

"Your uncle is right. He knows a lot about swimming. He made the Olympic swimming team when he was in college."

Meredith drew in her breath at hearing this, and exchanged a quick glance with Ward. A condition like Cullen's was certainly hard enough for anyone to bear, but for a gifted athlete it would be doubly hard. Thankfully, Meredith noticed that Maggie continued talking, unaware of her reaction.

"I wish Unk would go home with us, Daddy. I asked him to, but he said no. He could swim with me."

"We won't be filling the pool for another couple of months, punkin. It's colder in Tulsa than it is here." He placed food on his own plate and poured coffee for Meredith and then for himself. "We're going to enroll you in school when we get home, so you'll be very busy." He again met Meredith's eyes, then spoke to Maggie. "Merry is going to teach you some things that will help when you start school."

Maggie looked at Meredith with eyes big and round with astonishment. "Are you Mary Mary quite contrary?"

Ward laughed. The amber eyes gleamed at Meredith. There was nothing too familiar in his eyes, so she smiled happily back at him.

"My name is Meredith, Maggie, but call me Merry if you want to."

"I want to," Maggie said simply, and filled her mouth.

"Chew with your mouth closed, Maggie. I don't think Merry wants to see all that food rolling around inside."

The child looked at Meredith for confirmation, her mouth still agape.

"It seems to me that I remember seeing Princess Leia eating with her mouth closed." Meredith directed this remark to Ward.

He nodded gravely.

Maggie's eyes moved from one to the other. Abruptly she closed her mouth. When she emptied it, she said breathlessly, "Did you see her on TV?"

"No, in the movie. Do they show American films here?"

Ward answered for her. "There's an American colony in Chapala. They bring in American movies occasionally."

"Can we go see a movie, Daddy?"

"We'll see, sweetheart. We'll have to check and find out what's playing."

They were still sitting in the sunlit courtyard when an immaculately dressed man appeared — dark-skinned, dark-haired, with bold black eyes. He was certainly one of the most handsome men Meredith had ever seen, very slim and not much taller than herself. Almost a Latin version of Paul, she thought. With some relief, she realized she was not at all susceptible to his showy good looks.

He stood before her, clicked his heels, then with a barely perceptible bow said, "My name is Luis Calderon. *Buenos dias, señoritas. Buenos dias,* Ward."

"Morning, Luis. Help yourself to coffee."

"Gracias." He bent close to Maggie. "How are you this morning, my beautiful

one?" His voice was an exaggerated whisper and Maggie giggled.

Ward glanced at his watch and asked drily, "What brought you out so early, Luis? As if I didn't know."

The bold black eyes smiled into Meredith's. She felt irritation tinged with embarrassment. He was giving her his complete attention, ignoring both Ward and Maggie while he gazed at her. Finally Ward spoke again.

"If you want to bedazzle Miss Moore with your Latin charm, Luis, do it some other time. I want to leave for the plant within the hour and I have things to do."

Luis looked stricken. "You have no romance in your heart. How can you look at such a beautiful woman and not feel *amor?*"

Meredith got to her feet silently and uncomfortably. Luis stood up quickly. Ward remained seated, a slightly irritated look on his face. Maggie's small hand found its way into Meredith's.

"*Señorita.*" Luis's face took on a sad, dejected expression. "Perhaps you would be interested in joining me to see the surrounding countryside. Lake Chapala is very beautiful, you know."

Before Meredith could answer, Ward got

to his feet. "Oh for God's sake, Luis! You've got the hunting instincts of a tomcat. She hasn't even been here twenty-four hours!"

Ward's curt words didn't seem to bother Luis in the least, but they did Meredith. She was quite capable of turning down her own invitations.

"Thank you, *Señor* Calderon. Perhaps some other time." Her smile was more friendly than she intended due to her annoyance with Ward.

Luis came around the table, seized her hand, and raised it to his lips. "I shall hold you to that . . . Meredith."

She tugged her hand from his, took Maggie's, and they walked away. "Shall we call on your uncle, Maggie?" she suggested.

Maggie led her into the interior of the house and out onto a long, screened veranda. Meredith could see, now, that the house was built in the shape of an H, with a front and back courtyard. When they reached the end of the veranda, Maggie broke loose and darted into an arched opening.

"Unk! Unky!" she called.

Meredith followed her through the door and stopped. The room was huge, and plants of every kind and description were everywhere — on the floor, on low tables,

46

hanging from stands, and lining the window ledges. They had obviously been arranged with care and the effect was lovely. Meredith felt as if she were stepping into a magical garden.

"Hi."

The wheelchair came silently across the tile floor. The slightly built man in it wore a mismatched jogging suit and a scraggly beard. Maggie sat on his lap, her small hand working the controls of the battery-driven chair.

"Hi." Meredith smiled warmly. "Excuse my open mouth. I'm awestruck by this wonderful place. I'm Meredith Moore." She held out her hand.

He hesitated a moment before touching it briefly. "Cullen Sanderson."

He looked younger than Meredith had expected. His hair was lighter and longer than his brother's, but they had the same tawny eyes and sharp features. Cullen was handsomer, Meredith thought, or would be if he didn't have such a dejected slump to his shoulders.

"Can we show Merry the orchids, Unk?" Maggie squirmed around and looked into his face. "Please, can I show her my Margarieta?"

"I doubt if Miss Moore . . ."

"Orchids? Oh, but I would! I would love to see them. But we're not interrupting something, are we?"

"You're not interrupting anything."

Meredith followed the chair thinking he wasn't exactly enthusiastic about the visit, but she was determined not to allow that to dim her enjoyment at seeing his beautiful plants. Maggie looked back to see if Meredith was coming and almost ran the chair into a large fern. Cullen grabbed the controls.

"Watch where you're going, Maggie, or you'll upset us." He wasn't impatient or cross and Maggie giggled.

They went through a doorway and down a corridor. Meredith could feel the change in temperature. The air was damp and warm. When Cullen stopped the chair inside the door of a shaded, glass-enclosed room, Meredith moved past him. Along one side of the small room was a long bench with three slatted steps lined with pots of orchids. She was speechless. She had never seen anything so lovely. But that wasn't all. The other side of the room was a simulated jungle with tree trunks and vegetation growing from beds of moss and humus. Hundreds of orchids had attached themselves to the bark of the tree trunks and surfaces of rocks among the moss. The sight was stunning.

"They're beautiful! Absolutely beautiful!" She smiled into Cullen's eyes before he turned away.

Maggie slipped off his lap. "This one's mine, Merry." The plant was small and without a bloom. "I helped Unk divide it and next year I'll have a flower. I named it the Margarieta."

"Lovely! You'll have your very own corsage. I had one when I graduated from high school. My oldest and dearest friend sent it to me and I kept it in the refrigerator for days and days."

"Mine's going to be yellow," Maggie said proudly. "Unk said if we're careful the bloom will stay on for . . ." She looked at Cullen as if not sure of her information.

"About three months." He smiled fondly at the little girl.

"Do the blooms really last that long?" Meredith still found it hard to believe she was standing in a room full of growing orchids.

"They're not as delicate as you think. Like any other plant you grow, the requirements vary as to temperature, humidity, light, and moisture. These," he indicated the ones growing on the tree stumps and in the moss, "are the most common. They're called Cattleyas and are shipped by the thousands to the States because they are easily grown and the blooms last a long time." He wheeled his chair to the end of the room and turned a large water control faucet. A fine mist sprayed the growth. "They require a lot of water and plenty of ventilation."

Meredith moved to the door to allow the chair to pass.

Cullen reached down and plucked a large ivory bloom from one of the pots and handed it to her. Meredith's lips parted in speechless astonishment.

"Oh! Oh — you shouldn't have! It's beautiful. Perfectly lovely." She smiled into his upturned face and he didn't turn away. "Thank you. But," she protested, "I don't have a refrigerator to put it in."

He smiled this time with his eyes as well as his mouth, and she decided she liked him. He waited for Maggie to crawl back on his lap and they left the dampness of the orchid room.

"Would you like some coffee?" Cullen asked.

"I'd love some."

They passed quickly through the large room with all the plants and into a room cluttered with books, magazines, hi-fi equipment of every description, two television sets, a pool table, and so many other things that Meredith had a hard time taking it all in.

"It's rather mind boggling, isn't it?" Cullen remarked.

"Not exactly mind boggling, but very different from the rest of the house."

He helped Maggie off his lap. "It's a form of rebellion. Like letting your hair grow long. My mother hates it." Meredith wasn't sure if he was teasing. He moved his chair to a table, poured coffee, and passed it to Meredith. "What would you like, Maggie? How about a doughnut?" He opened a door beneath a long counter and brought out a plastic container filled with chocolate-covered doughnuts.

Maggie looked over the selection and picked the one with the most icing. Protesting "I really shouldn't" and "I don't need this," Meredith reached into the container when it was offered.

"You don't look as if you need to worry about your weight." Their eyes met, his amber and teasing, hers blue and shining.

"Not now, but there'll come a time when all this will catch up with me. While I was working at the hospital I walked a million miles a day and I could eat like a horse, but

51

now . . . I don't get half enough exercise."
Suddenly she realized what she'd just said.
Was that a callous thing to say to a man tied
to a wheelchair? Would he hate her for
talking about walking when he couldn't?
Their eyes met and she knew that he knew
what she was thinking.

"You can swim in the pool."

"Can't swim. I've only been in a pool a
couple of times."

"Unk'll learn you." Maggie licked the
icing from her lips. "Won't you, Unk?"

"You mean teach, sweetheart," Cullen
corrected her gently.

"I'd be hopeless," Meredith said quickly.
"I'd sink like a rock. Besides I won't be here
long enough for that." Then in order to
change the subject, she said the first thing
that came to her mind. "Your brother said
that you're a landscape engineer. It must be
very satisfying to create something as beautiful as the gardens here."

He shrugged. "It wasn't much of a chal-
lenge."

Maggie drew her arm across her mouth
leaving a streak of chocolate. "Can I have
another one, Unk. Please . . . ?"

Cullen surveyed her thoughtfully, a smile
curving his lips. "Go ahead, but you've still
got half a doughnut on your face."

Maggie jumped off the chair and went to him. He leaned over and she planted a wet, sticky kiss on his cheek.

"I love you, Unk."

"I love you too, sweetheart."

Meredith suddenly felt choked up, half on the point of tears. She had never before heard an open declaration of love between two people. It was so spontaneous, so sweet, so obviously sincere that she swallowed the lump in her throat and looked away.

"You'll miss Maggie when Ward takes her home." She didn't know why she said that.

"Yes, I will." The resignation in his voice touched her. She looked at him directly. His thin face was curiously reminiscent of Ward's. He had the same quality of reserve, but there was a sadness in his face that was lacking in his brother's.

Maggie finished her second doughnut.

"Go find Antonio, honey. Your face is all yucky."

Maggie scrambled away and Meredith took the opportunity to ask: "Who is that fellow Calderon? I just met him at breakfast."

"Luis runs our plant in Guadalajara. I call him the dude, but I guess he's an okay sort of guy." Cullen grinned. He had loosened up considerably since they first met. "I bet he's tried to *enamor* you already."

Meredith laughed. It was easy to laugh with him. He was nice. "Practice makes perfect and I doubt if *Señor* Calderon misses an opportunity to practice. Kidding aside, I appreciate being here and hope I'm not too much of an inconvenience."

"Not at all. Ward explained what happened in the hospital and I'm glad you're here. It's been so darn long since I've talked to an American girl." He looked away from her and out over the cluttered room.

"May I come back and visit you again?" Meredith desperately wanted to fill the void and save him embarrassment. "I was a shock to your brother, you know, and to the housekeeper, too. I think they thought because I'm an x-ray technician and unmarried I was a reject or something." She looked into his eyes with a conspiratorial smile.

"Ward isn't easily shocked."

"Who says so?"

The voice came from behind Meredith and she knew immediately who it belonged to. Embarrassment grew in her when she remembered what she had said. But — hang it all! It was true.

"Hi, Daddy." Maggie skipped into view. "We showed Merry my Margarieta."

"Did you, now?" He pulled up a chair and

54

sat down beside Meredith. "Here's a list from the school." He handed her a paper.

As soon as Meredith glanced at the list of five simple requirements, she knew that Jim had asked his cousin to create a task for her so she wouldn't feel awkward. She kept her eyes on the paper until she could gather her thoughts.

"May I see it?"

At his request, she passed the paper to Cullen. He looked it over and said, "She knows her ABC's and her colors, but she needs work on writing her name and tying her shoes. Can you count to twenty, Maggie?"

"I don't know," the child said indifferently.

Ward pulled at her braid. "We'd better get to finding out, pretty girl."

As Ward got to his feet, Meredith again noticed his height and slimness, emphasized now by his dark business suit. He looked down and caught her eye. Despite the glint of humor she saw there, there was something else, something reserved, private, that hadn't been there this morning. His eyes went to the flower in her hand.

"I'll leave you with Cullen and Maggie, Merry. See you this evening." He moved away, then turned back. "I'll tell Carmen to have the dinner served in the dining room, Cullen, so Merry can wear her orchid." He went through the door without waiting for a comment from his brother.

"Can I have a flower and eat with you, too, Unky? Please . . ." Maggie used her most appealing voice.

"You won't be able to stay up that long, sweetheart. How about a flower for you to wear while we have lunch?"

"Can Merry eat with us?"

"Sure. If she wants to."

Meredith grinned. Now that Ward had left them, the wave of self-consciousness had left also.

"I'd like nothing better."

"You have a very expressive face," Cullen said after Maggie had skipped away. "You have what my Spanish friends would call speaking eyes."

Her eyebrows lifted with interest and she smiled mischievously. "Don't tell me you can read my mind."

"Not quite, but almost."

"Thanks for warning me. When I get ready to steal the silver I won't think about it." She liked him, really liked him. He was easy to be with. The crackling tension she felt with Ward was gone now. Everything was right out there in the open. Meredith was pleased to see that there was even laughter in his eyes.

"I didn't mean that and you know it."

"I know it, but what did you mean, for heaven's sake?"

"Ward. You don't have to be afraid of him. If the truth were known, he's more scared of you than you are of him."

Her pulse gave an uncomfortable leap. "You're kidding!"

Cullen laughed at the amazement on her face. "No, I'm not kidding. It's a new experience for him to have a girl freeze up on him. Usually they fall all over him."

Meredith laughed nervously. "How do you know I didn't fall all over him . . . last night?"

"He told me. This morning. He said you were independent, stubborn to the extent that you would have foolishly left the *hacienda* because you took a dislike to him, and that you were stupidly proud."

Meredith sat very still and the grin left her face.

"I'm sorry," Cullen said quickly. "Have I embarrassed you? I guess I kind of got carried away. You see . . . it's been so long since I talked to a girl my own age."

There was such pain in his eyes when he spoke that it almost brought tears to her own. She reached out a hand to where his rested on the table and he turned his palm up to meet it.

"I'm not embarrassed, Cullen. It's a shock, I guess, to find out how you come across to other people. I've never thought of myself as being stubborn, or . . . stupidly proud. I have been foolish. Very foolish, in fact." There was a sad shadow lurking in his eyes. She caught only a glimpse of it and she came so near to telling him about Paul and her blind, foolish devotion to him that it almost frightened her. Their conversation was getting too serious. "Stupidly proud, am I? Well, your brother isn't the soul of diplomacy. There's something about the way he looks at me that gets my back up!"

Cullen laughed and released her hand. "He's a master at that. He's the only person alive who can make my mother back down. I feel kind of guilty at times because I don't help him with the business, but then again, since the accident I've at least kept my mother busy and off his back."

Maggie came in, trailed by a manservant. "Can I go tell Carmen we're gonna eat with you, Unk? Can I go pick my flower? Do I have to have a little one? Why can't I have a big one like Merry's?"

Cullen reached out an arm and drew the

child to him. "Maggie, sometimes I don't think your mouth and your brain are connected. How can I answer all those questions at once?"

"I don't know."

"Now about the flower. You can have a little one. Antonio," he called. "Let Maggie pick a Cattleyas. Then," he said to Maggie, "you can go and tell Carmen that you and Merry are going to have lunch with me." He wheeled his chair around and called out to Antonio again. "Hurry back. If we're going to have company for lunch, we've got to clean up this place and make it worthy of our guests." With this remark he winked at Meredith, then turned to the task at hand.

Chapter Four

It was nearly time for dinner and Meredith stood before the mirror, wondering for the hundredth time if the dress she had chosen was suitable. A blouson in butterscotch gold, its peasant top was gathered at a banded neckline. The full raglan sleeves were elasticized at the wrist as was the waist of the blouse. The material was soft polyester. The label inside the dress said, "machine washable-tumble dry." The only thing it had going for it, she thought wryly, was that it was soft and feminine and the color was right. She had no doubt the orchid she pinned to it would cost much more than the dress had.

That afternoon she had written a long letter to Maude Fiske, the social worker who had taken Meredith to the orphanage after her mother had been killed by a hit-and-run driver. All these years, as Meredith was shuttled from foster home to foster home, Maude had provided a sense of permanence and stability. She had been careful to keep a small box of personal belongings for Meredith and had visited her on Christmas and holidays. Along with Jim Sanderson, Maude was the closest thing to family that Meredith had, and Meredith knew she would want to know about the unusual events that had brought her to this magnificent *hacienda* in Guadalajara, of all places. Before she sealed the letter, she asked Carmen for the address of the *hacienda* so Maude could write her.

"To your *familia?*" the housekeeper asked, indicating the letter.

"No. To a dear friend."

She asked Carmen if she had a family. The question opened the way for a full hour's visit. Meredith discovered the estate there at Chapala was a lettuce ranch that employed a large number of people all under the direction of Carmen's husband, Carlos. She and Carlos had three daughters; two were married and one was going to medical school in Guadalajara. The servants in the house were well-trained, but needed supervision, Carmen explained. The *Señora* Sanderson was reluctant to leave her home unless she, Carmen, came in to see that everything ran smoothly.

"I enjoy being here when *Señor* Ward is here. He is much a man." Her dark eyes flashed, then narrowed as she looked at Meredith's unresponsive expression. "No?"

"Oh, yes. He's very nice." How could she say, she thought, that he scared her to death?

"Ward give you a bad time, eh?" Carmen, her eyes warm with sympathy, spoke with the familiarity of a friend rather than an employee.

"No. He has a right to know about the people he takes into his home."

"Ward is not a hard man. He may appear to be so. He is a much important man. I've known him since he was a small boy."

Feeling a little guilty about discussing her host, Meredith listened while Carmen told her how Ward had taken over the running of the numerous family holdings when his father died. His grandfather on his mother's side, though an American, had adopted Spanish ways and was in some ways more Spanish in his thinking than the beautiful *señorita* he had married many years before. It was a great disappointment to them when their only daughter married an American and went to live in Tulsa. She had died young, when Ward was barely ten, and the youngster began spending vacations with his grandparents.

During those summer months the old man was harsh with the young boy and was determined to make him into the Spanish son he never had. As much as Ward loved his grandparents, he couldn't forget he was an American and was torn between two conflicting lifestyles. On the high plateau in the mountains south of Colima on the Rancho de Margarieta, named for his beloved wife, the old man bred bulls for the arenas in Guadalajara and Mexico City. It was here on the rancho that Ward, saving his grandfather's life when he was attacked by a dangerous bull, was himself gored, resulting in the injury that left his leg permanently damaged. After the old man died, Ward gave up breeding for the ring and turned the compound into a cattle ranch where sleek steers roamed on the undulating pampas grass. Now he divided his time between the Rancho de Margarieta, the lettuce ranch at Chapala, Tulsa, and the plant in Guadalajara.

"Ward is much loved by the people on the *ranchos*," Carmen said with twinkling eyes. "Much of the *señoritas, americanas,* too. They all think they catch the rich husband." She laughed. "*Dona* Margarieta have different idea. She want him to marry with a Mexican girl and get a great-grandson before she die. Francisca Calderon, Luis's sister, is her favorite."

Meredith reflected on what Carmen had told her about Ward as she prepared for dinner. So his mother had died when he was old enough to miss her. She did understand him a little better, now, but pity him, she did not. She would be a fool to feel a moment's pity for such a self-assured person. Neither did she feel any pity for Cullen. She had seen many people with more severe handicaps doing much more with their lives.

Always having had to work, even as a young teenager, to help support herself, she simply couldn't feel much sympathy for someone who was content to sit in a chair and be waited on. She wondered what it would take to jar him out of his lethargy. Was it the fear that he would be unable to lead a normal sex life that had made practically a recluse out of him?

She caught herself up sharply. What was she thinking about? Maybe he wasn't interested in sex. Paul certainly hadn't been. During the three years of their relationship they had had sex exactly four times and, as far as she was concerned, the whole messy business was vastly overrated. At first she had wondered if something was wrong with her that she failed to excite Paul beyond a few kisses. She remembered the time she had ached with the need for him to make love to her and dared to take the initiative, only to be told firmly he wasn't in the mood. She had been utterly devastated. Never again, she vowed, would she set herself up like that for rejection.

Meredith waited in her room until ten minutes before nine, when dinner was to be served. Should she be on time? Should she leave her room now — or in five more minutes? What if Ward and Cullen dressed formally and what she was wearing was totally wrong? She stood beside the window and tapped her foot nervously on the thick carpet. And then, abruptly, she went to look in the full-length mirror. The dress was awful! Maybe if she did her hair up she would look less like a high-school girl ready for her first date. Quickly she brushed her hair up and secured it, pulled a few tendrils down at the nape, and looked at herself critically. That wasn't right, either! A soft knock interrupted her glaring at herself in sheer frustration.

She pulled open the door and there he was. Ward smiled at the surprise on her face.

"Why so surprised? I live here, too. Remember?" Just as they'd been that afternoon, his eyes were warmer, more friendly than last night. "I don't know how you managed to jar Cullen out of his rut, but he's waiting downstairs. He's even got himself all spiffed . . . up." The words died out as, all of a sudden, he was looking at her strangely. She wanted to go into the closet and hide.

"What's the matter?" she asked, forcing her tone to be light. "Have I got egg on my face?"

"It's your hair. You're not the suave, urbane type. It makes you look jaded, brittle, cynical." Was he teasing? He couldn't be flirting with her!

She tried to laugh. It wasn't much of a success. "Perhaps I am jaded, brittle, cynical."

He laughed and she decided again she liked his eyes. "No. You're refreshing, soft as a marshmallow, and . . ." He tilted his head and studied her. "And . . . whimsical."

"Whimsical?" Did he think she was a feather-brain?

"I should have added stubborn, argumentative, and late for dinner. Brush out your hair so we can go." He moved into the room. "Come on, Cullen's waiting."

She looked horrified. "Do you do this often?" What a rotten thought to pop into her head! She hoped he didn't.

"Ask women to take their hair down? Of

course not. Sometimes I do it for them." He was grinning broadly. Could this be the same man who almost threw her out of the house last night?

"Stop that!" She was grinning broadly, now, too and stopped his hand as he reached to pluck away a pin. She had already made up her mind to take it down, but decided to resist a while longer.

"Well . . . ?"

"Okay. But if I look like a mess it'll be your fault."

"You couldn't look like a mess if you tried."

"You're totally . . . unpredictable."

"And you're wasting time."

She removed the pins and her hair cascaded to her shoulders in a golden wave. She turned to the mirror and carelessly ran the comb through it. He was behind her and she looked into the tawny, smiling eyes reflected in the mirror.

"I was right." The satisfied look on his face made her sorry she had given in so easily.

"Are you always right, Mr. Sanderson?"

"Not always, Miss Moore. I didn't think marshmallows could bite." There was mischief in the tawny eyes. Without thinking, she allowed him to take her hand. "Hungry?"

"Starving," she admitted. And suddenly she was no longer worried that she might hiccup at the table or use the wrong fork.

Ward didn't release her hand until they walked into the room where Cullen sat waiting. Quite different tonight, he had chosen to wear a white, pleated shirt opened at the neck, dark trousers, and dark leather oxfords. His hair had been trimmed and the beard shaved from his thin face, making him resemble, more than ever, his older brother. As they entered the room, Meredith was pleased to find herself in an old-fashioned study. An oil portrait hung above the fireplace, in a heavy gilt frame. The strong-featured man depicted was, despite his white hair and somber black suit, so like Ward and Cullen in features as to be startling.

Ward followed the direction of her glance. "Our father."

Meredith thought about remarking on the striking resemblance between the half-brothers, but decided they might think she was being too familiar.

She was surprised to hear them discussing what had been in her thoughts. "You look more like him than I do," Ward was saying. He turned to her. "Don't you agree that Cullen looks like our father, Merry?"

Ward was standing in front of her holding out a glass of sherry. As she took the glass, his warm fingers encountered her own. His eyes were as friendly as before and she dismissed the silly notion to act reserved. She looked at the two men, then to the portrait, and back at the two men.

"You both resemble him, but — he was much better-looking."

Ward looked at Cullen and toasted him with the last of his drink. "Just what we need, brother. A smartass!"

Cullen laughed in pure disbelief at his brother's words. Meredith laughed with him. They were playing, feeling each other out, she realized with pleasure. She hadn't been so relaxed or had so much fun . . . in a long, long time. She wasn't breathless or blushing any more. She loved being here, being accepted for herself.

Cullen made a joke about escorting Meredith to the dining room and she placed her hand on his shoulder and said, "Lead on Macduff." The chair moved smoothly and she complained that she should have brought her track shoes.

They reached a long room illuminated by a crystal chandelier and diffused lighting from wide opaque panels in the ceiling. It was a pleasant mixture of old and new, the kind of room that created an instant illusion of warmth and welcome as well as luxurious living. The table was long and heavy, and the high-backed chairs would easily seat a dozen guests. There were three places set at one end. Cullen waited until Ward had seated Meredith before he moved his chair to the end of the table. She remembered the orchid and smiled into his eyes questioningly.

"Did I pin my flower in the right place?"

The eyes, lighter and more twinkling than she had seen before, smiled back at her. "No. It should be snuggled down in that gorgeous hair." He studied her seriously for a few seconds. "In that curve just under your left ear."

"Now you tell me. I don't have a bobby pin."

Ward got up and came toward her. "I'll fix it. I've got a paper clip in my pocket."

"You two are — nuts! You don't go with these elegant surroundings at all." She felt foolish as he fumbled with her hair and stirred restlessly.

"Be still or it'll fall in the soup."

Meredith had to look at something so she looked at Cullen. He winked at her! What was he thinking? Was it that she was going to hop into bed with his big brother?

Ward took his place across from her and called out to Sophia, who was hovering in the background. "We're ready now, Sophia. Serve the soup."

This particular miracle of having dinner with two attractive men and feeling quite worthy of their attention made Meredith glow with animation. The ball of conversation was tossed from one to the other and when it was in her court she was as glib of tongue as she had ever been in her entire life. She didn't stop to weigh words or thoughts as she chatted easily. When the meal was over Ward tucked her hand in the crook of his arm and they followed Cullen to the library, where a fire blazed gently. The tray with the chocolate pot was on the table beside the chair.

"Chocolate? Whose idea was that? What's wrong with an after-dinner drink?" Cullen made a face at Ward as he said the words.

"I ordered it for Merry. Whipped cream to go in it, too."

"More cream!" Meredith exclaimed. "I'll be as big as a tank, and have high blood pressure, heart disease, diabetes, cirrhosis of the liver, atherosclerosis . . ."

"But — rounded, jolly, and soft as a marshmallow."

Meredith still couldn't believe these

71

teasing words came from the man who last night, in this very room, had been so stern, so unyielding. A retort failed to come to her lips and she glanced at Cullen. A smile was playing around his mouth and she directed her remark to him.

"It isn't funny, Cullen. What red-blooded American girl wants to be referred to as a . . . marshmallow?"

He laughed. "You can be my marshmallow any day, Merry. A merry marshmallow!"

"Hush! You're making me self-conscious."

Ward had moved to the liquor cabinet and returned with a glass for himself and for Cullen.

"Drink your chocolate, Merry. We may persuade Cullen to play his guitar for us."

Later, in Cullen's room, she sat on the couch beside Ward and listened to the most beautiful music she had ever heard. Cullen's fingers danced over the strings and to Meredith it was like watching a ballet. She didn't know what she had expected, possibly a little diddling around with a ballad like "Greensleeves," but Cullen played magnificently. She didn't recognize the tunes but they were hauntingly sad in places, throbbingly passionate in others. She sat enthralled, not knowing when he finished one piece and started another. One song was so stirring that tears misted her eyes and she turned to see Ward looking at her. His hand came out and covered hers where it lay on the seat between them. She wasn't the least embarrassed for him to see she was moved by the sonata. She turned her eyes away feeling peaceful, content to let her hand remain beneath his.

The marvelous days continued, and she felt all the while as though she were suspended in time. The hours she spent with Cullen and Ward were both wonderful and strange for a woman who had never known family warmth before. The three of them acted as if they were very old and dear friends, visiting, teasing, playing cards or pool, listening to Cullen's music. She never allowed herself to think of Ward's life outside the *hacienda.* She didn't want to think of him as a wealthy man directing large corporations, but only as Cullen's brother and Maggie's father. And once, when he didn't return from Guadalajara, she and Cullen spent the evening together. That was pleasant, too.

"Do you use crutches, Cullen?" The words embarrassed her as soon as she said them.

He didn't answer for a long moment. "Sometimes. Why? Do you want to dance?"

"No, you jerk. I want to see how tall you are."

"I'm not as tall as Ward."

"Do you drive?"

"Yeah. Ward had a van fixed up for me. I don't use it much."

"Will you take me for a ride sometime? I don't want to leave Mexico without seeing something more than the inside of this *hacienda,* as beautiful as it is."

"Ward will take you. I'm sure you'd prefer it that way. If you're too bashful to ask, I'll tell him."

"You do and I'll punch you in the mouth!"

Both of them laughed, but suddenly his eyes grew serious. "I know what you're doing and I appreciate it, Merry. But believe me when I say I'm resigned to my life here. It's easier, a hell of a lot easier, being here than being out there trying to act . . . normal."

"Normal? What's normal?" She sat on the couch and drew her legs up under her. "While I was working in the hospital, Cullen, I must have seen every abnormality there is. It never got to the point where it didn't bother me. I tried not to let it show, but one patient who was blind *and* paralyzed from the neck down detected a note of pity in my voice and said to me, 'Hey, sister. Don't feel sorry for me. I've got a good brain and I've got my voice, that's more than some people have.' You know, Cullen, he had the voice of an angel, a beautiful tenor voice that gave him and many others a great deal of pleasure. I'll never forget him."

"And the moral of the story is . . . there's always someone worse off than you." Cullen picked up the guitar and began to sing. " 'Oh, Ru—by, don't take your love to town.' "

"Are you mad at me?"

"Kind of. But I'll get over it." He looked up and grinned. "You're as obvious as a tank."

She was relieved. "At least you can't accuse me of beating about the bush. You should be out there, living. You're very good-looking, you should be out there working, meeting people, maybe falling in love and getting married, having kids. There's nothing to stop you." She waited for him to tell her to bug off, but he started strumming the guitar again. Presently he looked up. The sadness in his eyes affected her more than any words he could have uttered.

"I'd like that, too, Merry, but why dream about the impossible?" His voice was very soft.

"You can't have children?" It was none of her business if he could have children or not, but for some reason she wanted to know. She already cared for this man like a brother. The hurt look on his face told her a great deal.

"Oh, I could have children all right, but for that you need a woman and what normal woman would look at me now?"

Meredith determined to carry the conversation through. "That's just not true, Cullen. You're feeling sorry for yourself again. Is there a girl you would like to marry?"

He heaved a deep sigh and absentmindedly strummed the guitar. After a brief pause he looked up at her again. "There was."

"Where is she? What happened?" They exchanged a long look and Meredith felt tears behind her eyes.

"I told her to get lost." He looked away and then back into her eyes with tears hovering in the corners. "Merry! Don't feel bad, sweetheart. Hey — like you said, there's a lot of guys worse off than me. I can live with it." He held out both hands. "See — look ma, no feet!"

"That's not funny, Cullen!"

"Yes, I know it, but what the hell! Better to laugh than cry."

She wanted to take him in her arms and hold him, soothe away the hurt. He was the brother she had never had, the child in the hospital who was frightened, but desperately trying not to cry. She had known him only a few weeks, but she knew he was kind, sweet, and gentle, and was coping the best he could after a cruel kick in the teeth. Why was it always the nice people of the world who got the shaft?

The following morning Meredith went boldly along the garden path to the swimming pool. Under the terry robe she wore a swimsuit borrowed from Carmen's daughter. Cullen and Maggie were in the pool. Sophia and Antonio stood patiently along the edge waiting to assist.

"Merry! Merry! Watch me. I can swim to Unk." Maggie, arms flaying the water, moved the few feet and threw her arms around Cullen's neck.

"Good girl. That's more than I can do." Now that she was here Meredith had cold feet about getting into the water.

"Well . . . come on in," Cullen called and splashed her with a spray of water.

"Will you give me a lesson?" She was stalling for time.

"Sure, but I'm expensive."

"Then forget it. I'll join the 'Y'."

The next hour spun past crazily. He leered unabashedly at the great deal of skin exposed when she dropped the robe, but the look was so open and so friendly that it only made her grin. A short while after she took the plunge, Sophia took Maggie out and Meredith and Cullen played like a couple of kids. He maneuvered in the water as easily as if he had the use of his legs. With his hand beneath her back he showed her how to float. One time he dove between her legs and sent her beneath the water. She came up sputtering, wiping the water from her face with her hands.

"Show-off," she accused when she could talk, then she exclaimed, "Oh, Cullen, this is fun!"

"For me, too."

"Tomorrow, same time? Same place?"

"It's a date."

She got out of the pool and wrapped herself in the robe. She didn't wait to see Antonio lift Cullen to his chair. It was too soon for that. Maybe tomorrow or the next day.

At lunch, which was usually served about three o'clock, Maggie and Meredith sat on the floor beside Cullen's chair and ate hot dogs roasted over a charcoal blaze Antonio had set in the fireplace. They sang crazy songs and laughed a lot.

Maggie planted a mustard and ketchup kiss on Meredith's cheek.

"I love you, Merry Merry. You won't go away, will you?" There was such hope and longing in her voice that Meredith thought a few seconds before she answered.

"Not right this minute, but someday. And I love you, too." If only she could record that little voice and keep it with her always.

"Not tomorrow?"

"Nope."

"The next day?"

"Nope. But one of these days I've got to go back to work. I work in a place where sick people go to get well."

"If I get sick, will you stay?"

"You're not going to get sick!" Meredith tickled her ribs and wrestled her down onto the floor.

"Don't, Merry! Don't . . . don't . . ." Between the giggles and screams Meredith heard the magic words. "Don't . . . pee pee . . ." She released her and sat back. "Don't you dare, you imp!"

Maggie laughed and darted away. "I fooled you!"

"You — little imp! That's not fair! You cheated!"

"This has got to be the noisiest place in Mexico." Ward came in, amusement spread all over his face.

"Daddy!" Maggie ran to him and he lifted her up and kissed her before he set her on her feet.

"Hi, punkin. Am I invited to the picnic?"

"There's none left. We ate it all."

Meredith got to her feet. She wasn't as relaxed with Ward as with Cullen. It was always the same for the first few minutes when she was with him.

"Never mind. I don't have time anyway. I'm going to see old *abuela*."

"Can I go see grandmother? Can me and Merry come with you?" Maggie's voice was coaxing and she wrapped her arms around his legs.

Meredith flushed because his eyes were on her.

"Not this time. Next time I'll take both of you. Hey — you're getting mustard on me, you . . . wiggle-wart!" He moved her away from him and wiped her face with what Meredith suspected was a very expensive handkerchief. "Off you go, now, so I can talk with Merry and Cullen for a minute." He watched her leave. "I'm going down to the *rancho* for a day or two, Cullen." Meredith started to move away. "Don't go, Merry,

80

you're practically a member of the family."
He smiled.

Meredith liked Ward better when he was smiling and was grateful to him for making her feel at home. She wanted to tell him and Cullen that she appreciated being a guest in their home and how much she had enjoyed the past few weeks, but she didn't wish to be gushy, or boring, so she stood quietly, her hands clasped in front of her.

"Merry's getting to be a pretty good pool player, Ward." Cullen's voice broke the silence. "She'll be able to give you a good game by the time you get back."

"I won't be gone that long, brother." He looked teasingly at Meredith, his eyes going straight to the center of hers.

"Just be sure you come back," Cullen called after him. "Francisca just might get her hooks in you."

He turned his head and looked fully at Meredith. "That will never happen." He made the statement firmly and emphatically.

The look he gave Meredith caused a tingling to run through her to the very marrow of her bones. His look had been somber, and absorbed. There was purpose and intensity in his face. From nowhere the thought came to her that he wore his masculinity like armor. Though there was strength, muscle, purpose, and power in every line of him, she sensed an incredible softness inside, a center so tender that Ward would not expose it for fear of a mortal wound. The tawny eyes stared deep into her blue ones for an instant, and she wanted to reach out to this man, to comfort him. In that moment she knew that, all appearances to the contrary, he needed such comfort more than Cullen ever had.

Chapter Five

"Merry, wake up!" Meredith heard the voice vaguely through the veil of sleep. It had to be Maggie. Who else would run into her bedroom calling her by name? She wished her head would stop hurting so she could open her eyes. "Wake up, Merry!" As the voice called out again, the bed heaved and her stomach with it.

"Please, darling. Don't jump on the bed! Oh . . . my head! Move, honey. Hurry . . . I'm going . . ." She threw back the covers and got to her feet. She stood swaying while the room righted itself, then headed for the bathroom, conscious of another pain more severe than the one in her head. Each time she put her foot on the floor, pain shot through her. Tiny claws were tearing deep inside her stomach and she felt bathed in cold perspiration. She made it to the bathroom and, leaning over the commode, gave way to her nausea.

"Are you sick, Merry?" Maggie crowded in beside her.

Foolish question. Her insides were turning inside out.

"Yes, darling. Go play like a good girl. Okay?"

That sickening, spinning feeling was lessened somewhat after she emptied the contents of her stomach and she sat down and peeled the band-aid from the place just above her ankle that was throbbing as if it had a life of its own.

Luis had come to dinner the night before and afterward she had walked with him in the garden and they had sat for a while on the veranda. It was while they were sitting there that she had felt the sharp sting and thought a gigantic mosquito had found her delicious. After saturating the wound with disinfectant, she had covered it with the plastic strip and forgotten about it. She looked at it now with disbelief. It was red and swollen. Something was obviously wrong! Definitely more than an ordinary mosquito bite, it needed more attention than she could give it. She stood and that sickening, spinning feeling came over her again. Any second she was going to fall flat on her face. She wished she hadn't sent Maggie away. Hot packs! That was what she needed to draw out the infection. She sat on the side of the tub and allowed the hot water to flow over her leg and foot until she had to throw up again.

She gained some temporary relief and made her way back to the bed. She tossed and turned, her mind uneasy about the bite on her leg. If Sophia would only come in, she would ask her to get Carmen. She would know what to do. Oh. . . . She felt so strange — almost outside herself.

She slept. If Sophia came she didn't know it. She dozed fitfully. Her brain was clouded and her fevered head hot and dry. She woke to find herself shivering, her leg throbbing. The skin was tight and hot. She was lucid enough to realize she had to let someone know how sick she was, but she could barely raise her head from the pillow, much less make it to the door. Please, she moaned inwardly, somebody come! She couldn't remember a time when she felt so bad. She was almost too ill to care what happened to her. Feeling herself float away, she gripped her pillow tightly as the room swayed and dipped.

There was a knock on the door and a deep voice called to her. The words coming through the door were jumbled in a strange disorder. They didn't seem to mean anything. She put her hand to her forehead wishing the words made some sort of sense.

Who would be calling her from so far away? Was it Paul? No! "I don't want you, Paul!" she managed to call out. She only wanted to sleep, but someone was coming toward her. She waited until he got nearer, just in case she knew him. It wasn't Paul. Paul was not so tall.

"Ward?" The word came out a mere whisper. She fastened her eyes on his face in mute appeal. "I'm . . . so sick."

He was there. Right there beside her, taking her hand in his. His voice was gentle, but urgent.

"What is it, Merry?"

"Don't touch me. I hurt so." Her eyes were bright with fever and her lips trembled when she spoke. Afraid he couldn't hear her, she clutched his hand. "I've got an infected mosquito bite on my leg, but there's got to be something more wrong with me than that." Big tears rolled out of the fevered eyes. "I'm sorry to be such a bother, but I need a doctor."

He turned back the covers to look at her leg. She gasped when he picked up her foot, sending waves of agony through her. Seeing the angry red lines running up toward her knee, Ward swore softly and gently eased her foot back to the bed and covered her.

"You have an infection all right, Merry.

But don't worry — we'll get a doctor out to fix you up in no time." His face was near, yet curiously blurred. She closed her eyes with relief. Ward would take care of things. "Don't worry," he was saying. "Leave everything to me."

His gentle voice persisted in her mind. She didn't need to worry anymore. Ward had come and he said not to worry, that he would take care of things. She didn't bother to open her eyes when the tablets were placed in her mouth and she was raised so she could swallow them or when the cool cloth was placed on her head. Orders were being given in Ward's firm voice and she drifted away in a swirling mist, only to return as gentle hands slipped a clean, soft gown over her head.

"I'm sorry," she whispered. Speech was an effort. The thought seemed to travel a million miles from her brain to her lips, and finally when she voiced it, the words were so soft the man leaned over her with his ear to her lips to catch them.

"Just rest, Merry. The doctor will be here soon."

"Doctor? Yes . . . I need . . ." Her voice was weak and her breathing shallow.

"Don't talk. Just sleep until he gets here."

"Doctor? . . ." she murmured.

"Don't talk, Merry."

She wondered about being called Merry, but she was floating away again, light as a thistledown, floating right off the bed. She clung to the hand holding hers to keep herself from being swept away.

"It won't be long, now." Her hand was held tightly. She wasn't alone! Please, don't go away, she begged silently. Don't leave me alone.

Vaguely she knew there were people in the room. She opened her eyes and tried to focus on the person bending over her, but the effort was too great and she closed them again. With listless disinterest she felt the pricks of the doctor's needle and heard the buzz of voice. Pain wrenched at her when her leg was moved. She cried out and heard someone curse.

"Don't hurt her for God's sake!"

The words faded and she was half lost in delirium. She didn't feel very much after that and when the voices had all gone away she slept deeply and dreamlessly, holding fast to the strong fingers interlaced with hers.

She woke once, her mouth dry and parched. Before she asked for a drink of water, an arm lifted her and a glass was placed to her lips. The water was cold and good. She was laid gently back on the pillow.

"Go back to sleep. You're going to be all right."

Her groping hand searched for the fingers she had clung to earlier. She slept. When next she woke Sophia was sitting in a chair beside the bed.

"Buenos dias, señorita." Her broad face expressed her concern.

"Is it morning?"

"Sí. Dos dias, señorita." She held up two fingers.

"Two mornings have gone by? It can't be!" She lifted her head from the pillow. It felt as if it weighed a thousand pounds. "I feel like I've been kicked in the head by a mule!"

"No," Sophia said seriously. "You very sick. Doctor say you drink." She placed a straw in Meredith's mouth and held it while she sucked up chilled juice. She was dry. She knew she needed the liquid after the high fever, but it was an effort to even draw it up through the tube. There wasn't a bone in her body that didn't ache and she was having difficulty keeping her eyes open.

"Thank you for sitting with me, Sophia."

"I tell *Señor* Ward you awake."

"No. Don't bother him."

"You no like *Señor* Ward?"

Meredith opened her shuttered eyes to see a puzzled frown on Sophia's face.

"Of course I like him. I just don't want to bother him."

"He say tell him when you wake, *señorita,*" Sophia said stubbornly.

"All right. Tell him if you like." She was weary and wanted to go back to sleep. She closed her eyes, heard Sophia leave the room and close the door behind her.

Through waves of fatigue she came swimming back to a certain awareness. Her eyelids felt as if two weights were attached to each of them, but with effort she opened them and saw Ward standing beside the bed. From out in the never-never land her mind grasped one fact.

"You haven't shaved." It seemed perfectly all right for her to say that.

He sat down in a chair beside the bed. "Didn't you realize you'd been bitten by a poisonous insect, probably a spider or a scorpion?"

She knew it was not a rebuke, but weak tears filled her eyes. She tried to stop them, but she couldn't.

"I thought it was a mosquito bite. It puffed up like a mosquito bite."

"It was more than a mere mosquito bite, Merry. The doctor will be back this morning to give you another shot of penicillin." An experimental hand felt her forehead. "Your fever is down. Sophia will bring a pitcher of orange juice. Drink as much of it as you can."

"You got a bit more than you bargained for when you took me in, Ward. I'm sorry." Her lips trembled and tears ran down the sides of her face into her ears. She didn't know why she was crying. What was wrong with her! She was blubbering like a two year old.

"Yeah! You've been a real pain in the butt!" His face was very close and he was grinning at her. He picked up the edge of the sheet and wiped her cheeks. "You've been very sick, Merry. When you're better I'll tell you just how sick. Now go back to sleep and don't worry about a thing."

She couldn't have said anything if she wanted to. Instead, with uncharacteristic impulsiveness, she grabbed his hand and held it to her wet cheek for a short moment. Thank you. She didn't know if she said the words aloud or not, but she meant them with all her heart.

For the rest of the day she dozed intermittently. Every time she woke Sophia was there with the orange juice. The doctor came and she opened her heavy lids at the prick of his needle, then closed them and drifted into a heavy sleep.

When next she opened her eyes, the first thing she saw was a cluster of yellow roses. They stood in a vase on the table beside her bed. Everything was peaceful now. The bedroom lamps diffused a soft, warm glow and the curtains were pulled across the windows. She stirred in a soft warm nest and her body felt curiously light. Her eyes traveled around the room. She was alone. Sophia's voice drifted in from the slightly opened door, then Maggie's pleading one. A smile touched Meredith's lips because she knew Maggie was giving Sophia the full treatment.

"The *señorita* is sleeping," Sophia said firmly.

"Please, please, pretty please, Sophia. Just one look before I go to bed. I'll be quiet. I promise." The little voice was soft, wheedling.

"I'm not asleep," Meredith called.

Almost before she got the words out of her mouth the door opened and a small body hurled itself into the room.

"Merry, Merry. I've something to tell you! Guess what? Guess what?"

"Don't get on the bed," Sophia scolded.

"Have you been good for Sophia?"

Sophia looked at the ceiling in a gesture of impatience and a torrent of Spanish words fell from her mouth. Meredith had a perfect understanding of what she meant, although the words were strange. She smiled and hugged the child leaning over her.

"What's this big news that's making you so excited?"

"Daddy said someday I was going to have a mommy! One all my own that won't go away."

The smile stayed on Meredith's face but the sparkle faded from her eyes. "Hey — that's great! That is big news."

Maggie was so excited that she bounced onto the bed before Sophia could stop her, and the sudden jar of the bed caused pain to shoot up Meredith's leg and she winced in spite of herself.

"You hurt the *señorita!*" Sophia grabbed the wiggly child and started for the door. "It sleep time, little mule."

"Bye, Maggie. I'll see you in the morning."

The door closed and Meredith allowed her face to rid itself of the set smile it had been holding. For the tiniest moment she felt terribly disappointed. It was insane. She was glad for Maggie. It was only . . . well . . . she hadn't thought Ward was even thinking of getting married. Francisca! Whoever this Francisca was she had evidently got her hooks in, as Cullen had expressed it. What was it that Ward had said that last evening? He had said something like, *"that will never happen."* He must have changed his mind.

A desperate feeling of loneliness possessed her, a loneliness that was her future. Turning on her side, she looked at the yellow roses. Lifting a hand, she gently stroked the fragrant petals. It didn't occur to her to wonder who placed them there, it just seemed they belonged . . . but she didn't. Her eyes roamed the room, taking in the beautiful furniture, the rich draperies and carpet, the outward manifestations of wealth. An abundance of love was the only wealth she craved, and if love were riches, she was most certainly a pauper.

The thought sickened her and she had no appetite for her dinner. She merely picked at the food and Sophia, coming back to collect the tray, looked at it disapprovingly.

"I did the best I could," Meredith said with a smile of apology, and Sophia carried the tray of scarcely touched food from the room.

When Ward came into the room, she knew by the look on his face that he had inspected the tray Sophia had returned to the kitchen. He came to the side of the bed and stood looking down at her. The weight Meredith had lost while sick gave her an ethereal fragility, and as the light tan she had acquired faded, her skin took on a translucent quality which made her eyes appear an even deeper, darker blue.

"Your tray was scarcely touched. Couldn't you have managed a little bit more?"

"Maybe later. It all seemed to stop here." She placed her fingers beneath her chin.

"The more you eat the sooner you'll get your strength back, *pequeña.*" His eyes sought and held hers.

"Yes, doctor." The tawny eyes were having the most disturbing effect on her senses. The tip of her tongue moistened suddenly dry lips. "I wish you wouldn't call me names I don't understand." She hadn't meant to sound cross but it came out that way.

A faint smile touched his lips. "What do you think I called you?" His eyes lingered on her mouth as if fascinated by it.

The sound of the softly spoken words sent shivers along her spine and she had the strangest curling sensation in the pit of her stomach that was fear or apprehension, she couldn't be sure which. Making an effort to control the situation with humor, she gave a nervous little laugh.

"Dingbat?" She felt a small triumph at speaking the word so lightly.

He laughed now and pulled a chair up close to the bed and folded his long length into it. He studied her for a moment, then reached out one finger and slowly traced the soft outline of her mouth.

"The word I used was complimentary. You must learn to speak Spanish if you want to know everything I say. I can swear better in Spanish than in English."

"I remember." She smiled, and he did as well, also remembering.

"Maggie has missed you. Cullen, too."

"It's nice to be missed." She looked relaxed, but her brain was spinning. All sorts of wild thoughts were whirling around in her head. She wanted to say, "Are you going to marry Francisca?" Instead she said, "What bit me to make me so sick?"

"It could have been one of many things. Mexico is full of poisonous insects. The house and gardens are sprayed periodically and I can't understand where you picked one up. It could have been serious, Merry. Why didn't you let Carmen or Cullen know? They would have called the doctor immediately."

"I woke up so sick I could hardly make it to the bathroom to throw up. By the time I realized something serious was wrong with me, I couldn't get out of bed." At the remembered feeling of helplessness she wanted to cry. "Thank you for coming when you did."

Lying there small and still, with his eyes on her, her pulse began to hammer heavily. A strange sense of awareness of him sent a warm glow through her whole being. She looked at him with eyes unconsciously wide and appealing. For a moment neither one said anything and it was as if the two of them were frozen there in time, waiting for something to happen. She moistened her lips with the tip of her tongue again and did her best to meet his censorious gaze.

"You're so damn polite you make me sick!" It was just the right thing for him to say to break the tension and she grinned at him.

"I thought you'd never notice."

Ward began to pace around the room, stopping to move aside the curtains so he could gaze out the window. She again noticed that, for a man so tall and with an injured leg, he was extraordinarily light on his feet. Meredith felt panic grip her as she realized that he might marry soon and she would be out of his life forever. Cold sweat broke out on her forehead and her heart hammered in restless dismay. Her alarm was mirrored in her eyes and he turned abruptly and looked at her.

"Did I frighten you about the bugs and spiders?" He came to the bed and picked up her hand and held it in both of his. She pulled her hand away, grateful he couldn't read her mind. "I'll send Sophia in to help you get ready for a good night's sleep. Tomorrow or the next day, or when you are feeling up to it, we're going to have a good long talk about your past, Merry. And . . . your future."

He went to the door. With his hand on the knob he turned around. "I don't know if there *is* a Spanish word for dingbat." He waited to see her grin, then went through the door and closed it softly behind him.

Chapter Six

Meredith slept fitfully throughout the long night. Her mind refused to allow her to rest. Try as she might, she could not fully assimilate the words Ward had spoken to her. Her future. It could only mean some arrangements were being made for her to leave the *hacienda*. Words, thoughts, emotions, all whirled around in her mind. Morning came and she was tired, but her leg felt much better. She could move it without pain and she longed to get out of bed and get dressed.

After Sophia removed the breakfast tray, she admitted a visitor.

Luis came in almost staggering under the burden of an enormous basket of fruit. He placed it on the floor beside the bed, his dark, sensuous eyes filled with concern. He grabbed Meredith's hand and lifted it to his lips.

"*Niña! Mi poca niña,* what have they done to you?" His words were soft and caressing and she couldn't help but to laugh at his dramatic expression.

"It was a mean old spider that did it. I'm all right now."

"If there is anything I can do, you just have to ask me," he said with a flourish.

She smiled warmly and shook her head. He made a grimace and sat down.

"I detest independent women," he said with mock hauteur. "You must learn to be clinging, submissive."

She forced herself not to laugh. "How arrogant of you! Women are not submissive anymore."

"You think not, *mi poca americana?* Spanish women are submissive and they love it."

"American women are not, Luis. They demand equality with men."

Luis lounged back in the chair. "I have pity for the American girl. All that freedom . . . and for what? She opens doors for herself, lights her own cigarettes, rides on motorcycles, and turns her bedroom into a public room. Poor American girl! Spanish girl is happy with a man who will curb her foolish ways, who will rule with a strong but gentle hand, cherish and revere . . . and master her."

"Do your Spanish women surrender without a struggle?" Meredith asked teasingly.

"No, *niña*. We enjoy our scuffles. They are like the chili pepper on the tortilla." He selected a plump peach from the fruit basket, produced a knife and proceeded to peel the fruit. "My sister, Francisca, is such a woman. She has been trained from birth to be wife, mother, and mistress to her husband. She lives with Ward's grandmother on the Rancho de Margarieta. It is Dona Margarieta's fondest wish that she and Ward marry."

Meredith watched the slender brown fingers, knowing his eyes were more on her than what they were doing. Instinctively she knew he was telling her this for a purpose. But why? He sliced off a portion of the peach and handed it to her, then served himself. They ate the fruit in silence. Luis was wiping the juice from her lips with his handkerchief when she raised her eyes to see Ward standing in the doorway. Unaccountably she felt color come up her neck and tint her pale cheeks.

Briefly she met his eyes and found their expression as much speculative as curious, one brow raised as if he were waiting for her to speak. She said nothing and he came slowly into the room.

"You seem improved this morning." He ignored Luis and stood at the foot of the bed.

"Yes. I'm getting up this morning." She flicked nervous eyes over him. Why did she suddenly feel as if he were the enemy?

"Rest in bed this morning. Maybe by late afternoon you can get up and sit in the chair." There was no *if* or **maybe** about it. He merely issued the order and her resentment grew. She should know when she was able to get up. She opened her mouth to say so, but he had turned to Luis.

"For the first time since we opened the plant we are behind in production. How come?"

The direct question caught Luis off guard. He returned his handkerchief to his pocket and got to his feet. There was a moment of silence, and Meredith's heart began to beat rapidly as she sensed the tension between the two men. An atmosphere charged with discord had pervaded the room.

"All the computer lines are right-on schedule — we're only behind in the electronic chess." Luis's voice was tight.

Ward persisted. "And why is that?"

"You know why, Ward." Was Luis going to lose his temper? Latins were notorious for that. "When you returned from Japan with the contract for the computer transistors, you knew it would put a strain on our production. The electronic chess game had to take second priority, as the other games were ready to be assembled." Meredith was surprised to note that, in talking business, Luis seemed to have lost much of his Spanish accent.

"It will be on the market for this Christmas season." There was a cold sting in every word Ward uttered.

"I do not think a lady's bedroom is the proper place for this discussion." Luis was angry. "Perhaps we can meet later."

"Then you will have to cancel your trip to the Rancho de Margarieta to talk strategy with your sister." There was a slight, cynical on Ward's lips.

"*Sí,*" Luis said softly, politely. There was a tone of mock deference in his voice. When he spoke again it was to Meredith. His face was smiling, his dark eyes devouring her. He picked up her hand and brought it to his lips. "Don't fly away from me, little *paloma.* I'll be back when you are feeling fit again."

Ward stood watching, his face a mask of immobility. Somehow he reminded her of Paul, silent and critical. Paul had looked at her in just that way when she had displeased him. She didn't want to be reminded of Paul.

"*Adios,* little pigeon." Luis released her hand.

"Thank you for the fruit." Meredith called to him as he reached the door. "The basket is beautiful."

Luis smiled. He was his most charming self again. *"No estan bella como usted, querida."* He laughed softly as he left the room.

Desperate to break the ensuing silence, Meredith asked, "What did he say?"

"He said, not as beautiful as you, darling." Ward lifted one eyebrow. Then he was laughing. His face was transformed, his cheeks creased and small crinkles appeared around his eyes making him look years younger. She wanted to punch him.

"What's so funny?" She kept a lightness in her voice as if it didn't matter that he found her amusing, but it did.

"I was laughing at Luis. Sometimes I want to wring his neck, but I do admire the way he can turn on the charm when he wishes."

He was looking down at her with amusement and she wished fervently she had the nerve to slip the sheet up over her head so she didn't have to face that mocking stare. She glanced quickly at him and then away. She heard the soft tread of his footsteps as he crossed the deep piled carpet to the window. She hated to be lying in the bed while he was in the room. She looked at his back. He was as handsome and commanding from behind as he was from the front. Well . . . not quite. His eyes made all the difference. When they were unsmiling, his arrogance was unnerving.

The moment he turned and walked toward her she knew he had something on his mind. He came to the bed and sat on the edge of it. She forced herself to look into his face, although her heart was palpitating wildly. Her eyes were lost in his intent gaze and she hid her hands beneath the bedclothes so he couldn't see their trembling. He stroked a strand of hair behind her ear, where his fingers lingered, their tips against her earlobe.

"Do you think you're in love with Paul Crowley?"

If he had said she had sprouted horns overnight she wouldn't have been more surprised.

"What . . . do you know about Paul?"

"You mentioned him when you were delirious. Are you in love with him?"

"No! But if I were, it wouldn't be any of your business!"

He smiled down at her, his teeth glimmering against his dark skin.

"I didn't think you were in love with him,

but I wanted to hear you say it." He removed his hand from her ear. "Are you content with your life, Merry?"

"What do you mean?" she asked, mystified.

"Do you ever wish for a home, a family, and security?"

She was silent, her eyes stunned and wide. She didn't like this personal conversation. She didn't want to talk to him about her private dreams. The silence between them was deep while she hastily gathered her confused thoughts.

"I'm no different from anyone else. I suppose that's what most of us want."

"I'm an impatient and busy man, Merry. And I realize that sometimes I'm not a very kind one. But when I make up my mind about something I like to act as quickly as possible. I think it would be to your advantage and to mine if we were married. How does the idea strike you?"

She looked at him as if he had just dropped from outer space. He was looking calmly back at her as if what he said wasn't the most ridiculous thing in the world. Either he was out of his mind, she thought — or she was!

"It strikes me as insane. And I agree you are not a kind man to even suggest such a thing. You're not in love with me and I'm not in love with you." Yet as she spoke the words, she knew that, at least as far as her feelings were concerned, they weren't true.

"I know that. I wouldn't insult your intelligence by pretending that I was. I believe that people who marry on short acquaintance because they have fallen madly in love are taking a step into the unknown with possibly painful results. The smart approach, I think, is to grow into love with someone you respect. Someone with whom you share mutual attraction." He reached for her hand which had crept out from beneath the covers and held it in his large one. Leaning forward, he kissed her lightly on the mouth. "Did you find that unpleasant?"

"N—no." What was he doing?

"I found it very pleasant and I'm sure if I were lying there in bed beside you I could have done a much better job of it." His smiling eyes held her mesmerized.

She bit her lip, a hysterical desire to giggle suddenly overtaking her. "You're crazy. Do you know that? Just plain crazy!"

The smile left his eyes and he said rather impatiently, "Don't you want a home . . . children?"

"Of course I want a home. I wouldn't be

normal if I didn't." The impatience in her voice matched his.

"And children?"

"Yes, but . . ."

"Your own?"

"Of course."

"Then you're going to need a man to accomplish that feat," he said drily.

She looked at him steadily. "I want love and a happy secure home before I bring a child into this world."

He looked at her and then away. "You're wishing for that old-fashioned relationship between one man and one woman, Merry. To be honest with you, I think that storybook, idealistic love is doomed to extinction. How, in this society, can anyone pledge his entire life and future to one person when it's impossible to tell what the next day will bring?"

She put out an unsteady hand. "How can you say that? I must try for a relationship that will endure. I have to have something to hold onto in this crazy world!" She held his glance for a moment then looked down.

"You can hold onto me. I don't repulse you. I can tell that much."

The cool assumption stung. She glared up at him. "You must know that marriage between two people from different lifestyles, who scarcely know each other, wouldn't work. I — I'm surprised you would even think of such a thing much less suggest it. It's ridiculous! How could you possibly be considering taking me into your family? You don't know anything about me."

"I know everything about you. I know you lived in eleven foster homes from the time you were five years old until you completed high school. I know the names of the families you lived with. I talked with one of your instructors who told me you are a girl with high principles and ideals. You were invited to take additional training in Rochester, Minnesota at the Mayo Clinic because you were second from the top of a class of one hundred and twenty. While in Rochester you were . . . friends with a man named Paul Crowley. He used you while he took his internship in the hospital where you were working. You helped to support his expensive tastes. When he got the opportunity to climb the social ladder, he took it and threw you over. You were unhappy, and when the child-snatching incident provided a good excuse for you to leave town, you jumped at it."

While he was talking Meredith wished she could die. The bastard! That he could pick up the telephone and lay bare every private aspect of her life caused her to hate him. The intense silence that followed seemed to press the breath out of her, drain all coherent thought from her mind until anger took over. Her lips felt stiff and it took every ounce of her control to keep her voice steady.

"That is the most malicious thing anyone has ever done to me in my whole life! How dare you pry into my background? You had no right!" Tears of embarrassment and humiliation ran down her cheeks. That her life had been held up to ridicule by this man was the most demoralizing blow she had received yet. She would leave this place as soon as possible!

"Get out of this room. Go! Get out! Give me the courtesy of allowing me to dress in private! I wouldn't spend another day in your house if I was dying. You've no right to drag my life out for ridicule!" She was crying and the sobs were shaking her voice.

"That was the last thing on my mind, Merry. I most certainly am not ridiculing your life. You have conducted yourself admirably. All I learned about you convinced me more than ever that I want you for my wife. I want no secrets between us. You must realize I couldn't ask you to become a member of my family without knowing as much about you as I could."

"What did you think I was, for God's sake? A call-girl?" The anger was leaving her and she just wanted to cry. How could he ever know the lonely and hard spots in her life? She had been respectable, dammit! Dull, but . . . respectable.

"Of course not. You're a beautiful, intelligent woman with good taste and charming manners. You're a good influence on Maggie and Cullen. I believe you will be an asset to my home, spend my money with good taste and in return I'm prepared to take care of you, be a faithful husband and an attentive father. That seems to me to be a sound basis for a happy and lasting marriage."

"You make it sound like you're buying a dependable car with good mileage. When I marry it will be for love."

"Love is a word that is tossed about quite a bit these days, but doesn't seem to mean much. Frankly, I'm not sure I know what love is."

"I can't believe you!" Meredith's words echoed back to her, seeming to emphasize her solitude. "Why? Why do you want to do . . . this?"

"That's a fair question. I want Maggie to

have a mother. One that won't go away as she puts it. I want a home to come back to with more than a houseful of paid servants in it. I want companionship. I want a woman in my home to make love to and a son I can watch grow into a man."

"Then why don't you marry Luis's sister? He said it's what your grandmother wants."

He leaned toward her, giving her the full benefit of the anger in his eyes, but when he spoke it was calmly.

"I don't happen to like Francisca. As many hours as I will spend with my wife, I want one that I at least like."

"Am I to take that as a compliment?"

"That is the way I meant it."

A warmth ran over her skin, for he gave his words a sensual meaning. Her fingers tensed in his. As often on momentous occasions one notices and afterwards remembers irrelevant things, so Meredith's eyes fixed on the dark hair springing from the long open V of his shirt. She felt a curious kind of panic as if some proud wild creature was staring at her. It was a mad and fanciful image and she banished it. Her eyes fell helplessly to the hand holding hers, and the gold gleam of a watch at his wrist, from which dark hair sprang. The image returned and with it the fears and the loneliness. . . . She raised her eyes to his and thought about all that he was offering. She had only to accept him and she would be Maggie's mommy, the one that wouldn't go away. It would mean she would give up all her fanciful, sentimental notions of love and settle for a calculated union.

"I don't expect you to give me your answer right this minute, Merry. Think about it." Then abruptly he moved and gathered her into his arms. His mouth had found hers before she could turn her head. It was not merely a light kiss of affection. He kissed her as though she were a woman with whom he would share more intimate caresses. She felt his lips, his teeth, his tongue. She opened her lips to his as the intimacy of the kiss increased and felt a strange helplessness in her limbs, as if his sensuous mouth was absorbing her.

"We'll do all right together." His face was near, his eyes staring into hers. She was breathing fast and so was he. Her head was spinning. When he turned her face toward his, there was no triumph on his face or in his eyes, only concern . . . for her. She was unbearably aware of his closeness.

"Do you believe I can be tender? I have moments, Merry. I'm not always the bear." He whispered the words mockingly before the firm lips became silent and feathered light kisses along her brow, her temples, and down her jaw line to her throat and his arms curved and pressed her more closely to him. Ageless moments passed while her bones felt as if they were turning to water. Finally, when she thought she could not bear the longing an instant longer, his mouth took hers in a kiss that engaged her soul. His lips hardened, and her own parted under them, admitting him, submitting. She touched the tip of her tongue delicately against his mouth and felt him tremble. She wound her arms around his neck.

"We'll be good together, Merry. It's a start." The muttered words were barely coherent, thickly groaned in her ear as he kissed the bare warm curve of her neck, following it to her ear and back to the hollow in her shoulder, covering her skin with light, tantalizing kisses.

"I think you'd better go." The strangled voice sounded miles from her ears.

He cupped a hand behind her head and pressed hard fingers under the disarray of her hair and drew her flushed face into his shoulder.

"It was unfair of me to spring this on you now. I should have waited for you to get your strength back. Rest and I'll come back this evening." He stroked a strand of her hair behind her ear as he had done before and stood up. He seemed to be a mountain of a man standing over her. "Cullen would like to come up this afternoon if you feel up to it." He smiled. "He must want to see you. It's a real production getting his chair up the stairs."

"I'll feel up to it." She said it quickly. She wanted to see calm, earthy, sane Cullen.

"I'll tell him then."

He was gone. She was alone. She ran the tip of her tongue around the velvety inner-side of her lips as his had done minutes before and her heart gave a disturbing throb. Oh, God! Why did she suddenly feel like she was in the ocean swimming against the tide?

Chapter Seven

Ward's parting kiss left Meredith prey to a thousand conflicting emotions. At first she felt outrage that he would even suggest a marriage of convenience. Did he think she would sell herself for mere security? And yet, the burning memory of his embrace sent delicious tremors through her still feverish body. What was wrong with her? Ward didn't even believe in love — he'd been perfectly clear on that point. She didn't . . . she couldn't . . . love the man. And yet she found herself weighing the pain and disillusionment of the last few months, the loneliness she had known for most of her life, against the possibility of luxurious content as his wife. As she steadied herself in preparation for his evening visit, rehearsing a diplomatic refusal again and again, only a lingering doubt remained.

As Ward moved quickly across the large bedchamber, Meredith noticed an uncharacteristic agitation on his face, belying his confident stride. In a moment, he was beside her, larger than life, looking deep into her eyes.

"Well?"

The single word of inquiry exploded in Meredith's brain and for a moment she could not speak. The well-rehearsed words died in her throat as a wave of longing, almost violent in its intensity, took their place. In a barely audible whisper, she heard herself telling Ward that she would be his wife.

"Now I would like to tell you about Maggie," he said quietly, his tone newly serious. "Contrary to what everyone outside the family thinks, she's not the daughter of my sister Connie."

Meredith drew in her breath. "But —"

He held up a broad hand, silencing her. "Let me finish. I know that Jim told you a bit about Cullen's accident, that our sister Connie was killed in it. But let me start from the beginning. You see, Connie went a little wild for a while and bolted during her college years. She went out to Arizona and joined a sort of traveling commune. They wandered about aimlessly, looking for God knows what. During Cullen's last year of college he went out to try and straighten her out and became involved with a friend of hers. It was this girl who later gave birth to

Maggie. After the child was born, the girl died from an overdose of drugs. Connie brought the baby to me. She was sure the child is Cullen's. But before we three could have a family conference to discuss what to do, he was in the hospital and had all he could handle facing the fact that he would never walk again — and that Connie had been killed in the accident."

Meredith gasped. "Poor Cullen! How awful." She looked straight into Ward's eyes. Gravely, she shook her head. "But Cullen should know that Maggie could be his child. It might make all the difference."

"I mean for him to know, Merry, but he wasn't ready before, believe me. Now that he's starting to come out of his shell, I think he can handle the news. It'll be quite a shock, you know. Anyhow, I'm telling you now because in this short time I think I have come to know you very well. There may come a time when you'll have to give Maggie up and I don't want you to be hurt."

Was there warmth and concern for her in his voice? She saw in the deep, velvet look absorbing her that she had not been mistaken. But, she reminded herself sharply, he would naturally be concerned for her feelings, just as he was for Cullen's or Maggie's.

Love and romance, however, were not part of the bargain.

"Yes," she said more sharply than she intended, "it will be easier giving her over to someone else if I know beforehand."

He took her chin between his thumb and forefinger and, tilted it, looked down into her eyes.

"You've got plenty of spunk, Merry. I know this situation is not of your choosing, but you're making the most of it, aren't you? You're still dreaming of a prince on a white charger who will sweep you away to his castle where there will be no more heartaches, no more problems. Life isn't like that, Merry *mía,* as you well know. If there were no heartaches, how would we know when we are happy?"

His words stayed with her for a long time after he left her.

Meredith sat beside Ward in the Mercedes, shocked that the past week had flown by almost as fast as the landscape was flying past now. Later today she and Ward would be married in a small church in San Antonio with only Jim Sanderson and his wife as witnesses. Meredith was glad that Ward had sent his cousin round-trip flight tickets the day after his incredible proposal.

Having a kind, familiar face there would make the whole affair seem less fantastic.

If anything convinced her she was doing the right thing, it was Maggie. Because of her, life had taken on a new radiance for the child. Maggie was the leveler, the thing that helped Meredith keep things in proportion. They needed each other.

Ward stopped the car and pushed the button on the dashboard. The big iron gates swung open and she turned to watch them close after they had passed through. She looked eagerly at the countryside. It had been dark when she made the taxi trip from the airport and she hadn't realized the estate was so large. The bold landscape fascinated her. Nothing was blurred in this country. Everything was clear-cut and diamond bright, under a deep sky dotted with fluffy cotton-wool clouds.

"What will your grandmother say about . . . us?" It was a subject they hadn't discussed.

Ward answered her question openly and frankly. "I telephoned her this morning and told her. She is upset."

Suddenly the vibrant glow in the air vanished. Meredith felt slightly sick with apprehension. Her hands, clasped tightly in her lap, became clammy and she stared straight ahead, seeing nothing that actually existed. Seeing instead a blurred image of a faceless grandmother rejecting her.

"And Mrs. Sanderson, your stepmother, will she be upset, too?" She knew she was a glutton for punishment, but better to know now than later.

"Oh, yes," Ward turned to grin at her. "She'll rant and rave about my duty to the family and about whether or not your blood is sufficiently blue to mingle with that of the Sandersons. But remember this, Merry. Her opinion or anyone else's means nothing to me. I am my own person. I make my own decisions. I please myself."

Meredith leaned back in the seat and drew in a deep breath. She tried to force her mind to pay attention to what was outside the car. They were approaching a ring of low, flat-topped hills.

She started when she heard Ward's voice. "What's worrying you?"

"I was just thinking that Luis wasn't very happy about our marriage either."

"Luis wanted to be my brother-in-law. He's a very mercenary fellow. He can't stand his sister, Francisca, anymore than I can, but with her married to me his own personal fortune would have been more secure."

"Are you always so frank?"

"Not always, but I will be with you. I said I wanted no secrets between us."

They talked off and on after that, but impersonally, about the land, the birds, the flowers. They were going into the downtown area to pick up some papers Ward wanted to mail while they were in the States. Meredith commented on the beautiful flowers growing in profusion in the parkway. She had always loved flowers.

"Guadalajara has one of the most ideal climates in the world," Ward explained. "The temperature hovers between fifty-eight and seventy-two degrees the year round. Many Americans retire here." He braked sharply as they rounded a curve and waited patiently for a horse-drawn cart to turn off the avenue. They continued in silence for a while and then he pointed out *Aqua Azul* Park and the *charro* ring. He explained that the bull riding contest was held here.

"The contest is equivalent to a rodeo in the States. The only difference is that a *charro* brings a bull to earth by the tail rather than by the horns. I'll take you to one some time. They are very colorful."

"Do they have the bullfights at the same time?" If that were the case she would have to find an excuse not to go. She didn't believe she could bear to see an animal tormented and slaughtered.

"No. The bullfights are held in the bullring. An altogether different sport."

"Do you go to the bullfights?"

"Never. I don't care for the sport."

In the heart of the downtown area he pulled the car to the curb so that she might see the giant cathedral.

"They began building this cathedral in 1571 and finished it forty-seven years later. It's a magnificent building. When you stop to think that it was built eighty years after Columbus discovered America and without modern technology . . . what an amazing achievement."

They paused in front of an office building and a uniformed doorman darted out with a briefcase. Ward spoke to him in Spanish and they moved once again out into the line of traffic.

Meredith didn't wonder that people wanted to retire to this beautiful setting. Her eyes wandered over the shaded plazas, green parks, glittering fountains, elegant statues, and the carefully tended flower plots which were ablaze with the deep orange of marigolds, the scarlet of zinnias, and the crimson petals of roses. It was a modern city with trolleybus and taxis, yet horse-drawn carts also seemed strangely at home on the busy streets crowded with small foreign cars all darting in and out of the traffic lanes. She marveled at how they wiggled into the smallest space with only inches to spare on either side. At every traffic light there was a blast of auto horns. Ward laughed at the expression on her face.

"It would be impossible for a Mexican to drive without a horn."

She grinned back at him, and wondered fleetingly when the beautiful coach she was riding in was going to turn back into a pumpkin.

A guard tipped his hat as they passed through a private gate at the airport. They drove some distance around long, low hangers to where a silver white plane waited. Ward drove the Mercedes up to within a short distance of the plane and stopped.

They went up the steps to the plane together, but when they reached the door he stood aside so she could enter. It was like walking into a sitting room. There was a long low couch, tables, lamps, occasional chairs, thick carpet, and even a beautifully framed landscape on the wall. She turned to Ward. Quite suddenly she was aware of nervousness, of uncertainty, of a number of nameless doubts.

"This is yours? We're going to fly in this? Alone?"

He met her tormented glance with puzzlement before he smiled. "Not alone. The pilot is going with us."

She didn't smile back. "Then you really do live like this." She said it half to herself with a little sinking feeling in the pit of her stomach. Good Lord! What was she doing here? How could this be real?

Ward saw the serious, scared look on her face and placed a reassuring arm across her shoulders. "Are you afraid of flying?" He searched her face.

Meredith was not fearful about the short flight, but she was beginning to grasp the reality of Ward Sanderson's wealth. How would she bridge the gap from her world to his? She turned wide grave eyes to his face. How could she possibly stand beside this man as his wife? It would mean more than merely babysitting his child. She would have to direct servants, greet his guests, meet his business acquaintances. Her clothes, manners, all her actions would be scrutinized by his friends, his stepmother, the press. Oh God! She had forgotten about the press! Would they find out about the wedding? From what Jim had told her, everything the Sandersons did was news in Tulsa!

"Ward!" She looked at him now with a look that blended confusion and fear. "Let's talk about this. I'm not sure . . . I didn't think, didn't realize while we were at the *hacienda* that you were so . . . were so . . ." She didn't want to say the word "rich," but what other word could she say? "I didn't think about the kind of life you live. I should have thought this out more clearly. I don't usually let my judgment get so insanely out of hand. Surely you can understand now that you see me . . . here. I don't fit in! I've not been anywhere or done anything that would make me interesting to your friends. I've no experience, no . . . polish. I've never even given a . . . party!" Her voice caught on a sob.

"A party?" His arm tightened around her and his voice was sharp in her ear. "Who in the hell cares about a party? You're wrong about yourself, Merry. You'd be an asset to any man. You're you, Merry, and that's part of your charm. My life isn't as glamorous as you probably think it is. I have this plane because my work makes it necessary, not because I'm a jet-setter. And if you're worrying about managing my home" — his eyes glimmered — "wait until you've met Edna. She is the most infuriating, capable woman in the world. She runs the house like she was the master of a ship and spoils me terribly." He laughed. "I can't wait until she sees you."

"She won't like me any more than your stepmother and your grandmother."

"That's where you're wrong. She'll look down her nose, size you up, then take you under her wing and love you."

Meredith said nothing for a long moment, then turned tiredly and rested her forehead against his arm.

"If this doesn't work out, Ward, or if you meet someone, fall in love, and want to marry, this . . . arrangement doesn't have to last forever." Her voice was muffled and she felt stupidly close to tears.

"And if you should meet someone, you'll tell me? I'm hoping we'll be able to talk to each other about everything, Merry." He held her and swayed softly. In his arms, she felt safe.

Her answer was almost breathless. "I will. I promise I will."

Their eyes met. Hers were bright with tears, his gentle, questioning. It seemed both an end and a beginning for them. Reluctantly, she pulled away and sniffed.

"I don't cry all the time." She fumbled for a tissue.

"I'm glad to know that. I was beginning to think I'd have to order these things by the truckload." A handkerchief appeared in his hand and he wiped her eyes, his own bright with amusement. He urged her toward the back of the plane and into a small compartment. "We'll be taking off soon and there's something I want to show you." A number of boxes were stacked on the small bunk. Ward ignored them and slid open a door exposing a half dozen garments hanging on padded hangers. "Carmen selected some things. I . . ." The closed look on her face stopped him from saying anything else. He waited and her face relaxed and he smiled. "I knew you wouldn't have time to shop and every woman is entitled to a new dress to be married in, to put away in mothballs so she can drag it out twenty years later and see if she can squeeze into it. When we're airborne you can come in here and rummage around and select something."

Meredith looked down at the silk dress, her best, which Sophia had pressed for her. Now wasn't the time to allow pride to rear its head. Unconsciously she stroked a strand of hair behind her ear.

"Thank you."

Ward clamped his hands firmly to her shoulders and pulled her toward him. His kiss was quick and firm. He raised his head and grinned. His voice, when he spoke, was husky.

"I think that bears repeating."

His face came to hers and he kissed her longer and harder. The first time her lips had been compressed with surprise, but now they were soft and yielding. Her palms rested on his chest before they moved around to his back and she hugged him to her. He raised his head. They looked into each other's eyes and exchanged another smile. She was happy. God, she was happy! Back in the secret recess of her mind though, she knew it wouldn't last, couldn't last. It was too beautiful. When it ended she would adjust. . . . She always had. Voices forced her mind back to the present. The pilot was aboard and Ward was urging her gently back through the narrow doorway, to her future as his wife.

Chapter Eight

The sun shone warmly on Meredith's wedding day, its brilliance touching everything including the diamonds clipped to her ears and the magnificent pearl and diamond choker Ward fastened around her slender neck moments before they left the hotel room. She looked beautiful and stately as she approached the flower-decked altar in the large, almost empty church. Her trembling hand was clasped firmly in Ward's and he measured his steps to match hers as she walked in the new high-heeled pumps that matched perfectly with the soft gray cashmere suit that she wore. Ward was wearing a dark suit for the occasion with a small, violet orchid attached to his lapel. Meredith's bouquet was made of large violet orchids and Jim Sanderson's wife Ruth held a bouquet of beautiful yellow roses.

Ward had said he would take care of everything and he had. All Meredith had to do was choose her dress and sign her name to the marriage certificate. The ceremony itself was simple and the minister, an elderly man with wisps of gray hair combed over his almost bald pate, spoke his words solemnly.

"Dearly beloved, today we are gathered together in the sight of God and man to join this man and this woman."

It all seemed so unreal to Meredith, like Cinderella going to the ball. But this was no ball, she quickly reminded herself — it was her wedding day! This day she was joining her life to that of a rich, handsome, story-book prince charming. Would she wake up to find herself back in a foster home, with only a life filled with loneliness stretching out before her?

"Do you, Ward, take this woman to love . . . and to cherish . . . in sickness and in health . . . for richer, for poorer . . . till death you do part?"

Meredith's eyes went quickly to Ward's and found that he was looking down at her. His words, spoken firmly, echoed in the silent church.

"I do."

Meredith felt the impact of his words. *For richer, for poorer, till death do us part.* The circle of diamonds was being placed on her finger.

". . . I now pronounce you man and wife. What God has joined together, let no man . . ." The minister was smiling. "You may kiss your bride."

Ward bent down and brushed her cold lips with his, and took her hand and interlaced his fingers with hers. Suddenly, she was terrified thinking about the enormity of the step she had taken. How could Jim and his wife be smiling and Ward so calm? Oh, Jesus! She hoped when the time came for her legs to move they wouldn't fail her. They didn't.

The two couples moved out of the church and into the bright sunlight. Here everything seemed so normal. Traffic moved, horns blared, and children raced by on the sidewalk. They got into the car waiting beside the curb.

"It was a beautiful wedding and you were a beautiful bride." Ruth Sanderson was almost tearful.

"Thank you." Meredith managed her stock answer for almost everything. Her lips trembled and her eyes felt misty. She longed for a tissue to wipe her nose, but since her hand was still clasped in Ward's, and her other hand clutched the bouquet, she allowed herself a small sniff. Ward looked at her strangely and she willed her eyes to stay dry and her nose not to run.

They arrived back at the hotel where they

had met Jim and Ruth and where she had changed into her wedding clothes. The driver helped her from the car and then Ward's protective clasp took her to the private elevator that whisked them to their rooms. An elaborate buffet, including a bottle of champagne resting in a bucket of ice, awaited them.

The high heels of Meredith's beautiful pumps sank into the thick carpet. She felt more than ever like Cinderella. Ward had handled everything perfectly. They had driven from the airport to the parking ramp of this hotel, up the private elevator to the suite of rooms where Jim and Ruth waited. They had made the trip to the church and back without seeing anyone but the driver and the minister. Ward had shielded her from publicity as he had promised.

She stood beside the couch wishing desperately she didn't feel so nervous. If she felt shy, Ruth did not. She was plainly impressed with the elegance of the rooms.

"Isn't this room gorgeous, Jim?" She settled onto the rose colored silk couch. "Could you just imagine our girls when they were little sitting here on Saturday morning with a bowl of cereal in their laps and their beady little eyes glued to the cartoons?"

Jim laughed. "And you running around in one of your faded flannel nightgowns?"

Their laughing eyes met and held. A blast of envy struck Meredith. Jim adored his wife.

"I want you to know, Jim Sanderson, that I may never leave this place. We've had a regular little second honeymoon ourselves." Ruth spoke to Jim, but her twinkling eyes were watching Ward and Meredith.

"You'll leave, love." Jim loosened his tie. "A team of mules couldn't keep you out of the car when I head for the airport." He said it drily and winked openly at Meredith.

She liked them immensely, both of them, and longed to be like them, easy and relaxed. They were being themselves, honest, all agog at the splendor of this fabulous hotel. Her eyes went to Ward. He was watching her. Aware the tawny eyes were on her, she bit her lower lip, searching for something light and clever to say. Dammit! He knew how nervous she was.

"Tired, Merry?"

She met his eyes. "I guess so."

He gave her a sudden, gentle smile and the tawny eyes glowed warmly. He came toward her, lifted the bouquet from her hands, and placed it on the table. When he moved away from her to the cocktail cabinet, a chaotic rush started to whirl in her brain. She was married to this man, yet she hardly knew him. Though she felt that she was living a novel — rich man meets and marries poor girl and takes her to his mansion where she lives happily ever after — she now realized that her naive romantic ideals had allowed her to be fooled by Paul. All of a sudden she knew that most of her life she had floated around in a romantic mist, but now she had to face facts. She was in love with Ward! The words beat against her mind. It had taken a long time to recognize the signs that had been there for the noticing. The way her eyes seemed to be constantly drawn to him, the pleasure she felt when she looked at his tall erect body, the secure, protected feeling she had when she was with him.

She felt a sudden, delirious rush of joy. She had fallen completely, utterly in love with the man, the real man behind the figurehead that was Ward Sanderson. How could she bear knowing that he did not love her?

He came to her just at that moment and put the cold glass in her hand. The magic ended. She came back to reality with a jolt. She felt her cheek go paler. Evading his eyes, she took the glass and would have turned away, but his free hand caught hers. She looked up and met dark amusement in his eyes.

"Jim, you and Ruth come and drink a toast to my bride."

Meredith found it difficult to concentrate on what he was saying. Try as she would, she couldn't think of anything but the realization of what he meant to her. You're in deep water, Meredith, a voice inside her warned.

Time went fast. Then Ward moved discreetly into another room in the suite so Meredith could speak with her life-long friends. Jim and Ruth hugged her warmly goodbye. "I wouldn't have missed this for the whole world, Meredith. I suppose you know by now that I'm really a romantic at heart." There was an affectionate smile on Jim's face. "I think Ward got himself a super bride."

"I'm not sure I could have managed without you and Ruth here — it all happened so quickly. To think that if it weren't for you, Jim, I might never even have met Ward, no less married him. . . ." Meredith shook her head in disbelief.

Jim's face grew somber. "So you do love him! I'm glad. Frankly, I was worried about that. More than anything, I want you to be happy. And Ward needs love almost as much as Cullen does."

"How is Cullen?" Ruth quickly interjected. "Have you been able to get close to him, find out what he's thinking? Is there anything you can tell me that I can take home to my sister?"

At Meredith's puzzled look, the older woman explained her remark. "My sister Becky has been in love with Cullen since they were sixteen. They became really close after the accident in spite of his mother's efforts to keep them apart. Then suddenly Cullen told her to get lost. It almost killed her. She has moped around for two years now doing nothing but work with her quarter horses and play her guitar. I wish there was some way they could get together. Is Cullen any better? Has he made an effort to do something with his life?"

"I've only known Cullen a few weeks, but Ward seems to think he's beginning to come out of his spell." For the first time in her life a feeling of belonging enveloped Meredith. She belonged to Ward, now, and Cullen and Maggie were family. "Cullen spends a lot of his time with his flowers and his music. He plays the most stirringly beautiful music I've ever heard. He seems to pour all the longing in his soul into it. Tell your sister he's lonely. If she loves him, she'll have to make the first move. Cullen feels he has nothing to offer a woman."

"I'll tell Becky what you said. She cares about him a great deal."

As the two of them moved closer to the door, Meredith said quickly, "I'll keep in touch. I appreciate your being with me today. I don't know how I can thank you."

"You already have. You've given us news of Cullen," Ruth said. The two women exchanged a hug and Ruth regretfully shrugged into her jacket. "Have a great time in Acapulco."

"We will."

Ruth hugged her again, and then she and Jim left. There was a tug at Meredith's heart as she walked slowly out of the room behind her. Ruth was a beautiful woman, beautiful inside where it mattered.

After a few suggestions from Jim on how to handle a wife and a playful exchange of banter, the door closed behind them. Ward reappeared.

There was silence.

"Well, Mrs. Sanderson?"

Meredith tried to remain calm. "Well, Mr. Sanderson?" The small laugh she tried refused to come convincingly. Her throat was tight with nervousness and she wasn't sure she could say anything more without betraying the fact to him. Soundlessly he had moved to put his hands on her shoulders and turn her to face him. Her heart gave a choking, little thump and she raised a tremulous gaze to his face.

"You were very beautiful today. No man could have been more proud of his bride than I was."

Her lashes dropped and her cheeks felt warm.

"Blushes, Merry? I do believe you're genuinely without vanity. What other virtues have I yet to discover in my wife? Patience? Modesty? Not meekness . . . I know that!" His brows came together, then raised in amusement. "I suspect you have unexpected depths, Merry, Merry, quite contrary. And before many weeks have passed I will have explored every single one of them."

She stood there, silently, watching him. He took her hand and led her to the bedroom door.

"I'm taking a shower. How about you?"

She nodded and went slowly into the bedroom.

"Which bath do you want? The pink? I'll take the brown. Don't use all the hot water."

Could he be nervous? Making small talk

to cover up? His teasing words didn't go with the look on his face. She glanced at him in the mirror. He had taken off his coat and was in the act of removing his tie. His hands were steady, his expression guarded. He caught her eye in the mirror and she quickly averted her gaze and removed the clips from her ears and the necklace from her throat.

While she ran her bath and undressed, she wondered how many women Ward had slept with and how often he would expect to make love to her. Her sexual experiences with Paul had only left her feeling frustrated and used. She looked at her naked body, reflected from every angle by the mirrored walls of the bathroom, and the thought that it was no longer only hers, but Ward's as well, to touch and caress, sent a violent thrill through her. And he was hers. As if seized by a fever she brushed her teeth, tied her hair back and sank down in the tub to hide her nakedness.

She bathed, toweled herself until she was properly dry, and fought out a crazy mental dialogue with herself all the time. What did he expect from her? The thought of that big bed made her fingers and toes feel icy cold despite the steamy heat of the room. In the mirror her eyes were wide and darkly brilliant. The woman reflected there looked like a stranger.

She slipped the prim blue nightgown over her head. This was her wedding night and she was going to bed with her new husband in an old, five-dollar nightgown from the discount store. Abruptly she turned away and forced herself to be calm. She dabbed skin fragrance on wrist and temples and walked back into the bedroom.

Ward lay on the bed, his hands behind his head, a single sheet pulled up to his bare chest. He eyed her without moving. She sat down at the dressing table and picked up her hairbrush. While she was desperately thinking of something to say, he spoke her name, the one he had given her.

"Merry."

Her face was pale when she looked at him. She looked directly into his eyes and her mouth went dry. Her eyes flicked over him and hurried away. His bare shoulders had a silky bronze sheen to them and his chest was deeply tanned, but roughened by dark hair that grew down the center of it. A wild, sweet enchantment rippled through her veins and wordlessly she got up, went to him, and put her hand in his. He moved slightly and made room for her to sit beside him.

"Merry." When he said her name again it was a caress. He ran his hand up and down her arm. Finally he said, "I want you to want me, Merry. Anything else leaves me cold. I won't insist if you're not in the mood."

"No, Ward . . . it isn't that, I . . ." she whispered, her voice faint, her breathing ragged. "I'm willing to be a wife to you . . . in every sense of the word."

"Willing and wanting are two different words," he muttered in a hoarse, thickened voice. "If you need more time . . ."

Denial choked her throat. She almost wanted to cry. The knowledge that he wasn't trying to rush her into fulfilling an obligation brought its own welling of love, and tremulous joy came like a pain, so great it was, and her heart began to race. He watched her with eyes that were dark and anxious and through them she sensed the langorous restraint keeping a rein on his passion. No words would come so she reached out a hand and switched off the bedside lamp and slipped into the sheets beside him.

His arms were waiting for her and pulled her trembling body against his. They lay quietly for a long while, until her trembling ceased. Then he began to stroke her, his hands uncovering her body slowly, achingly, until she lay naked, soft and warm beside him. Carefully he turned her face to him and kissed her long and hard, his mouth taking savage possession of hers, parting her lips and invading it in a way she had never imagined any man would ever kiss her. His hands were moving everywhere, touching her hungrily from her thighs to her breast. While he was kissing her the compelling hands stroked her breasts, and her nipples hardened. His fondling fingers generated their own heat as her naked desire mounted and set her trembling again.

"Sweet Merry. Sweet marshmallow Merry." His voice was thick, his lips touched the slope of her breasts, then down to tease the stiff nipples, caressing them delicately so that they hardened even more. His hand wandered down to the curve of her hip and stroked her thigh, his own thigh moving restlessly against her, his breathing faster and harder as he touched her.

He leaned over her, his breath warm and moist, his face a blur in the soft light. She wanted to caress him, to get to know his body as he was getting to know hers, and yet . . . the fear of rejection, of having him remove her hands from his body, nagged in her mind while she lay passively accepting his caresses. She could feel the tension building in him while her own body trembled and her lips longed to search for his.

"God!" he said bitterly, his hands gripping her shoulder. "Don't you feel anything?" He looked down into her face then buried his in the curve of her neck.

She felt her body tense, heard his intake of breath, and knew he was going to leave her. Her arms went round his neck, clinging. Her mouth touched his own so lightly it was like the brush of a lash on his skin. She breathed carefully, as though afraid she might frighten him away. Her hand came up and clasped his cheek, cupping it, holding it against her, and then the pressure changed. His lips hardened and her own parted under them, admitting him, submitting. She touched the tip of her tongue delicately against his mouth. They kissed hungrily, and explosive desire opened between them now.

"You want me . . . do you want me?" The muttered words were barely coherent, thickly groaned into her ear as he kissed the bare warm curve of her neck.

"Ward, Ward . . . I . . ." She didn't know what to say, afraid to put words to her fear.

He seemed to understand. With a swift look into her face he took her mouth again. He kissed her as openly and intimately as a man could kiss a woman. Her inhibitions left her and she arched against him, her hands moving over the smooth muscles of his back and down to the smoothness of his buttocks, aware of his tense excitement, listening to the heavy beat of his heart and aroused by the feelings she found in him. At least she was unafraid to let him know that she wanted him and when his husky voice groaned thickly in her ear she did not even try to decipher the muttered words. He might be merely a man who liked making love to women, and did not much care which one he took to bed, but it no longer mattered. She had never felt anything like the sensual enjoyment she was feeling now. Tonight she knew the excruciating drive to be satisfied. She moved against him, clutching at his back while he pressed into her. She wrenched upward and tensed, wanting to know and have every little bit of him. His weight pressed her slimness into the mattress, and her arms tightened about him as they rode out the storm.

When it was over he lay beside her and muttered, "Yes, yes," as if she had said something. Even in the dark she turned her eyes up to his in answer and he kissed her, slowly, sharing the moment of sweet tranquility with her. His arm left her and he reached to the wall above their heads and a softly fused light came on beneath the bed. He propped himself up on one elbow and looked at her. She sighed in contentment. In the soft cocoon of the bed her doubts and fears had dissolved, and her body drowsed, luxuriating in this new and wondrous sensation. He looked down at the pale luminous oval of her face framed in the tumbled hair that was soft and shining in his fingers.

"Your eyes have lights in the dark. Did you know that?"

She shook her head and raised a hand to his cheek. "Ward, I'm not very experienced." His hand stilled in the thick, vibrant hair. She felt a tension in him and hurried on. "I've done this only a very few times. Four in fact and I never . . . never really participated." Now that the words were out she only half wished them back.

He was still for a long moment before the hand in her hair moved to beneath her head.

"My God, what a bastard! That was why it took you so long to show any feeling. I thought that I might repulse you . . . somehow. " He pulled her close and held her for a long time. He whispered softly in her ear as she ran her hands over his back. "My pleasure is greater when I give you pleasure. Did you enjoy it?"

"Yes! Oh, yes!" She framed his face with her hands and reached for his lips. This moment was hers; nothing or no one could ever take that from her.

He peeled down the sheet and stooped to kiss her breast. He did it so gently that her whole body cried out for him. She lay back among the pillows feeling happier than she ever had before and he loved her again, tenderly, unhurriedly, caressingly, stroking and entering her again and again. Her hands spent the night learning his body. They said little, but it was one of those rare nights when bodies spoke silently and ignited and burned on for hours. It was almost dawn when he whispered to her, "Go to sleep, Merry. The sweetest sleep in the world comes now."

She found that it did. She fell asleep almost immediately, falling into a deep, satisfying slumber, but all night she was subconsciously aware of the warm, male body pressed to her own, the heavy weight of the arm across her body and the hand that cupped her breast. It was a wonderful way to sleep. She woke in a wonderful way, too.

"Wake up, sleepy head. We leave on our honeymoon in twenty minutes." Ward was leaning over her, his tawny eyes sparkling and alive.

Her yawn stretched into a smile and she stretched out on the comfortable bed. It was extraordinary! Exposing her body to him was like the freedom . . . to fly. She smiled and slipped her arms about his neck and ran her hand down his back.

"Wanton woman," he said intensely and gave her a lecherous smile. "Come take a shower with me."

"You're indecent!" she protested as he pulled her from the bed and they hurried, laughingly, into the bathroom and into the stream of water that seemed to come at them from all sides.

"My hair! What'll I do about my hair?"

"Leave it on your head. I like it there."

She laughed joyously. She would never have dreamed she could be this happy or that he could be like this. He seemed a thousand years younger, boyish, devilish, but considerate and affectionate, too. He pushed the wet hair back from her face and pulled her to him. She tilted her face to meet his kiss and the shower ran full in her face until his head shielded her from the spray. Under the warm water they kissed. She felt his arms tighten around her and his body press against hers. Suddenly she was as hungry for him as he obviously was for her. The water rained down upon them and they couldn't seem to get enough of each other.

He moved his head to look down at her and the spray ran full in her face again.

"I'll drown!" She giggled and leaned her forehead against his chest.

He grasped her shoulders and turned her back to him. "We must remember not to do this when we're in a hurry." He said the words softly and slapped a wet washcloth in her hand and poured a flask of fragrant liquid soap down over her breast. "Wash up. The porter will be pounding on the door at any minute."

Chapter Nine

Two surprises awaited Meredith in Acapulco. The first came when Ward drove the rented car they picked up at the airport into the long, wide drive leading to the Acapulco Princess Hotel. The massive structure stood like a pyramid among a tropical garden of palm trees, bright flamed poinsettias growing the size of shrubs, golden marigolds in sculptured plots and a profusion of red, mauve, and pink blooms that lined the drive dividing it from the carefully manicured lawn. It was a scene she had seen many times on travel posters, but in person it was much more beautiful.

"Are we going to stay here?" The note of awe in Meredith's voice echoed her feelings.

Ward's tawny eyes warmed as he looked at her. "I thought you would enjoy coming here. Perhaps another time we'll try one of those little, private cottages clinging to the side of the hill up there."

Meredith's eyes followed his gesture and saw the pink cottages, each with its own private pool and surrounded by lush green, terraced into the side of a cliff.

"If you'd rather . . ."

Ward laughed. "Next time. I wanted you to see this place. It's one of the most beautiful hotels in the world. It was on the top floor that the multimillionaire Howard Hughes spent his last days."

"Poor man," she remarked and then laughed with Ward at the irony of her statement.

The awe was still with her when they entered the massive hall where live trees, shrubs, and hundreds of blooming rose bushes thrived in spite of being surrounded by tiers of hotel floors. The lobby was crowded with hotel guests and, as they passed, Meredith heard French, German and a Scandinavian language. With his hand firmly attached to her elbow, Ward propelled her to the desk and then to the elevator. She had little time to think, but she could not help but notice the way her husband commanded attention, demanding service in a quiet, firm manner then tipping without appearing flamboyant.

The second surprise came in the form of a telephone call from Jim just as they were preparing to go out to dinner. Meredith moved about the room restlessly while Ward talked. When he finished he came to her and dropped a light kiss on her nose.

"You can forget your worrying, Merry, Merry. Mr. Thomas decided to drop charges against Laura Jameson. You and Jim were right on target — once he had time to cool off, he took pity on the poor girl. There's even a good chance that she may pull her life together and get the child back. Anyhow, Jim says to tell you to enjoy your honeymoon."

Upon hearing the good news, Meredith felt a warm glow of satisfaction. For the first time in her life, things were going to turn out right! And when Ward sensed her mood and suggested, "Let's go celebrate — how would you like to see the Mexican boys dive from *La Quebrada* tonight?" Meredith agreed with a happy grin.

Later, standing beside Ward, his arm tucking her close to him, they watched a young diver. Perched on a torchlit spot high on the side of a cliff, he raised his arms, leaped out from the rock, and dove, like a graceful bird, into the narrow ribbon of water far below. Meredith turned her face into Ward's shoulder, sure the slim youth would be dashed against the rocks.

"Wait until you see him dive from the very top of the cliff. It's about a hundred and twenty feet down and they must wait until the water is at least twelve feet deep in the gorge. It's usually about eight feet in that area. It's split second timing that's important. I've seen them dive dozens of times and it always raises the hair on the back of my neck. But these boys make their living this way and they know what they're doing." Like a father with a frightened child he turned her around in his arms. "Watch this, now. He won't get hurt. I promise you."

Atop the rock the youth intently, watched, the surging green water rush into the chasm, and he timed his dive to the rhythm of the incoming tide. Meredith released a pent-up breath as the graceful body sprang out, two blazing torches held in his outstretched hands. She watched until the lithe, arrow-like body sliced into the green water, and then she turned her face once again to Ward's shoulder.

"Is he all right?"

"Sure. Look at him scramble out of the water. They know what they're doing. Their work is probably safer than driving a taxi down *Costera Miguel Aleman.*" He looked down at her with warm, friendly eyes and she wanted to snuggle closer to him, but the show was over and people were turning

away from the plate glass window that over-
looked the chasm.

It was a honeymoon right out of a romantic novel. Although it only lasted four
days and four wonderful, glorious nights, it
was the kind of honeymoon that comes at
the end of the story when love triumphs and
the couple walk off into the sunset. These
thoughts came to Meredith as she packed
her suitcases. Ward had left the room reluctantly, saying he had a few things to attend
to before they departed for the airport.

Meredith had learned a lot during the last
few days about the man she had married.
She found that he was as hungry for affection as she was, and any time she voluntarily
put her hands on him he responded,
whether it was while they were making love
and she let her hand run over his chest or
while they were walking on the beach and
her hand sought his. At times she could hear
his heart thudding powerfully against hers.
At others, the warm light in his eyes and the
smile on his face told her more than any
words that he liked her to touch him. How
different he was from Paul who had avoided
any physical contact.

She also learned her husband could be
possessive and almost cruel at times. It was
as if he had two separate, quite distinct per-

sonalities in one body, the considerate, gentle man she loved — and the cruel, arrogant one who would whip with his tongue anyone who he thought was infringing on his privacy, or his property. That side of him had been demonstrated only that morning.

They had been sitting in the courtyard at a small table under a huge umbrella. Meredith was writing a post card to Maude, passing along the good news about the Jamesons, when Ward was paged to take a telephone call.

"I won't be long. Will you be okay here or do you want to come with me?"

"I'll stay here and enjoy the sunshine. I just can't believe there's snow and ice in Minnesota." She held up her hand, and he squeezed it before walking away.

For several minutes she watched the crowds pass, then her eyes caught a scene unfolding farther along, at a table set under a palm. A young Latin man had attracted the attention of a middle-aged American woman. Meredith presumed she was one of the idle, rich women Ward had told her about, a hint of distaste in his voice. They came here seeking a diversion denied them in their own respectable home communities.

She leaned back in her chair and closed

her eyes against the sun's fierce glare. When she opened them a tall, fair young man, with a smooth tan and direct, friendly eyes stood before her.

"Hi. I know it's an old line, but don't I know you?"

Meredith stared at him and after a moment came up with a smile. "No. I'm sure we haven't met."

"I swear I've seen you somewhere before. Was it . . . New York, Chicago, or San Francisco?" He laughed and moved to take the chair beside her. "A face like yours would be hard to forget." He was a handsome young man, dressed casually in expensive clothes. "I've covered the States. Was it the Riviera?"

Meredith had been guardedly polite, but the man's persistence began to annoy her. Was he one of those paid companions and lovers to deprived middle-aged women? She was neither rich or middle-aged and she wished he would go about his business.

"I didn't invite you to sit down," she said coolly.

Undeterred, he looked knowingly into her eyes. "Did your husband send you off to vacation alone?"

Meredith felt his gaze slope down over her body and realized with sudden, cold clarity that he was mentally stripping her. Anger surged along with sudden embarrassment, but before she could express it a shadow fell across her face and she glanced up in heart pounding panic when she saw the look on Ward's face.

"Merry!" The word exploded from him, low and hissed.

"Mary." The young man got to his feet. "That's the name I was trying to remember. I knew I had met you somewhere."

"You've never met her anywhere! Come near her again and you won't have the equipment to ply your trade!"

"Look here . . ." A flush came up in the man's face. Meredith didn't know if it was anger or embarrassment.

"You look here, Lothario." Ward said the word with an unmistakable sneer. "If you're too goddamn lazy to make a living any way other than taking bored women to bed, that's your problem, but stay away from my wife!"

"Who the hell do you think you are?" The young man's voice rose with indignation.

Meredith looked around. They were attracting attention. She got to her feet and took Ward's arm.

"I'm her husband, that's who I am! And if you don't want to lose your teeth, you'll get the hell away from here!" Ward was flaming with fury by the time he finished. Meredith's hand insistently pulled at his arm and he moved away with her.

They didn't speak a word until they were in their room and Ward turned to her accusingly.

"I'm not gone ten minutes and you engage some gigolo in chit-chat."

She flushed angrily. "That's unfair! I didn't engage him. He thought he recognized me."

"How stupid can you be? He took one look at that desirable body of yours and he thought he had it made. Good looking and rich, what more could he want?" He said it jeeringly.

The coldness of his tone was unbearable and somewhere deep in her heart a small hope died a quiet death.

"If he thought that, he was in for a big surprise. I don't have two *pesos* to rub together!"

"With you, money would have been secondary. Bed was on his mind!"

"And you have a nasty mind!"

"Maybe, but what did you expect? Did you think I'd stand by and watch you react encouragingly to a pickup?"

"I didn't encourage him!" Her eyes were sparking angrily at him.

He looked down at her, his tawny eyes dangerous. "You know damned well you did! He liked what he saw and you were flattered. Well, get this — you're married to me and I won't stand around watching you flirt with every Don Juan that comes along."

"If you thought there was any likelihood of that, why did you marry me?" Before he could answer the question, she rushed on. "All I did was be polite and you have me in bed with him!"

"If I really thought that I'd be breaking your neck by now." He said it softly and menacingly.

Their eyes met in a long, silent war. Her breath began to come fiercely and she desperately wanted to cry. Then he turned away and strode into the dressing room. She went into the bathroom, closed the door, and let tears slide down her cheeks.

Meredith managed to control her emotions. She faced the mirror squarely and with care, dreading the moment she would have to face him again. It came as soon as she opened the door. He was standing there.

"I was about to come in and see if you had floated down the drain. Ready for lunch? We've about time before we pack up to go." He smiled and the lazy charm of his glance took the edge off her nervousness.

"Sure. And I'd like a huge bowl of mixed fruit with that delicious green dressing." Their eyes held and she smiled. He looked at her closely then lowered his head and kissed each eyelid as if kissing the tears away. She knew that this was the nearest thing to an apology she would ever get, but, nevertheless, it was enough. His hand moved down her arm and grasped hers. She interlaced her fingers with his.

Chapter Ten

A little more than an hour after the plane left the Acapulco airport it landed on the Rancho Margarieta. A dust-covered jeep, driven by a Mexican in white, baggy pants, came out to meet them. He embraced Ward as if he were a relative and when Ward introduced Meredith, the man took off his straw hat and bowed low before striking Ward a blow with the hat and bursting into laughter followed by a stream of Spanish that set Ward to laughing, too.

When they reached the *hacienda,* the jeep stopped outside the walled courtyard and they walked through an arched gate. Brick-paved and dotted with trees, shrubs, tubs of flowering plants, and graceful fountains spewing cool water, it was like an oasis in the desert. The house had thick walls with arched doorways leading on to wide verandas. Hanging baskets of flowers were everywhere. Meredith hardly had time to take it all in before Ward urged her forward and into a wide tiled hallway where they were met by a very old woman in a long black dress.

Again Ward was hugged like a favorite son. He gently kissed the wrinkled cheek and introduced Meredith. Alert, bright eyes looked her over before a huge smile appeared. She embraced Meredith much the same as she had Ward. Meredith was both surprised and touched.

"Saldana has been with my grandmother for many years. They are about the same age." He explained this to Meredith, then spoke more slowly to the woman. "Is my grandmother well, Saldana?"

She made a gesture with her hands. "Ah . . . *si,* sometimes. We are not young like you, my young stallion." Her eyes twinkled up at him and she smiled an almost toothless smile. "It is *siesta* time. Take your bride up to rest. I will tell your *abuela* that you have brought your new *esposa* to her. Do not be surprised if she is angry." The old woman laughed. "But not as angry as Francisca, no?"

Saldana's frankness caused questions to swirl through Meredith's mind. How was she going to face this hostile grandmother? Would she feel, once again, like the unwanted child thrust into a foster home? Pride surfaced. No, by damn! If the old lady didn't like her, tough!

Later while waiting in an unfamiliar room for him to come for her, some of her bravado faded. The room itself was intimidating, its tall, mirrored doors reflecting the monstrously large bed positioned between narrow windows. The bed had high lofted mattresses covered by a woven spread of coarse white cotton which emphasized the darkness of the Spanish bedroom furniture and the highly polished wood floor. The room would be fitting for a Spanish bride. Had Ward's mother been conceived on that large bed.

Just then Ward came into the room without knocking, and she welcomed his intrusion into her thoughts.

"Ready?" He looked her over, smiled, and reached out to tuck a strand of blond hair behind her ear.

She had dressed carefully in an apricot silk dress with a short jacket and flared skirt. She had applied a minimal amount of makeup and when she looked at her reflection thought she looked plain and washed-out compared to Mexican girls with their midnight black hair and white skin.

Trying to be flip to cover her nervousness, she flashed up at him what she hoped was a confident smile. "Ready for the lion's den," she replied.

"It won't be that bad." His eyes searched hers and there was such a tender look in them that her heart lurched crazily. "She's disappointed that I didn't marry a Mexican woman, but when she gets to know you it will be all right. She's really a softy where I'm concerned. You'll see."

"I hope so." She slipped her hand into his and her confidence came dribbling back.

But her uneasiness returned as they walked down the broad, carpeted steps. What thoughts were going through his head, she wondered? Had he seen Francisca? How was she going to bear up under the strain of living with him, knowing he only liked her, was more than satisfied with their sexual relationship, but didn't love her? At any time he might meet someone and fall in love! Would she be able to bow out gracefully? Would the decision she made to marry him demand more of her than she would be able to bear?

They came to high, double doors and Ward put his hand on the ornate knob. She looked up at him imploringly.

"Just be yourself. You look beautiful," he murmured.

They walked into a cool, quiet room. The ceiling was high and fans with thin, wide blades whirled slowly and noiselessly, stirring the air. Heavy, high-backed velvet upholstered chairs, square tables, and a long, low couch decorated the room. At first Meredith thought the room was empty because the small lady in the dark dress sitting on the large chair blended with her surroundings.

With her hand firmly clasped in his Ward led her forward. He bent and kissed the old lady's cheek.

"Here she is, Grandmother. I told you she was beautiful." His voice was soft, almost reverent. There was a gentleness about him when he looked at this small, wrinkled woman.

Very dark, bright eyes looked steadily at Meredith and she looked steadily back. Instinct told her this woman would look with contempt on any one who stood meekly, passively, under her stare. Her features were small beneath jet black hair threaded with silver. It was wonderfully thick hair, piled in soft swirls atop her proudly held head. Her hands were slender and well cared for and gripped the arms of the chair as if she were about to rise up. The silence dragged on as the two women looked at each other, and Meredith realized she was going to have to speak the first words. She pulled her hand from Ward's and held it out to the woman who sat so stoically.

"I'm glad to meet you, *señora*." It seemed to Meredith she held her hand out for ages before a hand came out to meet it. The clasp was firm but didn't linger.

"Sit down." She was still looking at Meredith and her words were more of a command than an invitation. Meredith walked back a few steps to an identical high-backed chair, but before she sat down the woman said to Ward, "Leave us." Her voice softened only a fraction when she spoke to her grandson. Meredith's eyes flew to Ward's. He came to her and slid his arm across her shoulders. His eyes told her he wouldn't go if she wanted him to stay. She moved out of his embrace.

"I think your grandmother and I should get to know one another on a woman-to-woman basis, darling. Do you mind?" She sat down in the heavy, straight chair, her feet just comfortably reaching the floor.

"Not if that's what you want, sweet-heart." He bent over her and looked into her face before he dropped a kiss on her cool lips.

"I'll be fine." She mouthed the words to him while his face blocked his grand-mother's view of her lips. His hand lingered on her shoulder and he squeezed it reassuringly before walking away.

A calmness had come over Meredith. She looked at a sliver of sunlight on the floor and heard the soft sound made by Ward's closing of the door. She looked into the cool, dark eyes and smiled. Lady, she thought, you would be surprised to know how many times I've sat in a hard, straight chair and faced a stranger who had the authority to dictate my life. Never again. I'll meet you on equal terms. Whether we shall be friends or not is up to you. She knew Ward's grandmother was waiting for her to say something, but decided to let her steer the conversation into whatever channel she chose. When she did speak it was to the point.

"I wanted my grandson to marry a Mexican." The words were firmly and calmly spoken.

"I know. Ward told me."

"He has roots in Mexico. Obligations here."

"I'm sure he does."

"American women do not strive for family unity. They are interested only in being liberated from what they consider dominance by their husbands or male counterparts." She spoke sharply, accusingly, and with scarcely an accent.

Meredith sat quietly realizing the *señora* expected her to debate her statement.

"I'm sure you have certain reasons for your opinions, *señora.* Some American women are so dedicated to getting equal rights for women that they seem to have forgotten that the core of every great nation is family solidarity. Each family unit must have a head, which doesn't necessarily mean a woman is any less equal than her husband. They only have separate functions within the family."

"Submissiveness is not an American trait."

"That is true. However, submissiveness means different things to different people. To me it means yielding to authority, and for this world to survive we must have authority. To others it may mean admitting to being inferior, being humble, meek, submitting oneself to dominance without any effort to control ones own destiny. The latter meaning does not apply to me, *señora.*"

The *señora's* face gave no inkling of what she was thinking. The dark eyes continued to look at her. She was a true aristocrat, Meredith decided.

"Do you love my grandson or did you marry him because he is rich?"

The question caught Meredith unaware and she sat for a moment before she spoke.

"*Señora,* I didn't know when I married Ward what it was like to be rich. I have never had money so how was I to make a comparison? I will tell you frankly that I married him because I yearned for someone of my own, a family. You see, I have no living relatives that I know of, and Ward's proposal was very tempting. Since the wedding I have come to love him very much. He is the man I dreamed about when I was a child — kind, loving, dependable, protective. The fact that he is rich just happens to be an added factor and can very well be more of a hindrance to my happiness than a benefit."

"I want him to be happy. He tells me he loves you. I'll have to accept you."

"Thank you, *señora.* I'll try not to be a disappointment to you. I want Ward to be happy, too. I hope that can be a basis for a friendship between us."

"We will have coffee." The old woman took a small, silver bell from her pocket. The musical sound was soft but must have reached the ears of the young girl who pushed a noiseless teacart into the room.

"This is Leticia, Saldana's great-granddaughter."

"*Hola.*" The girl kept her face turned away

and Meredith barely heard her whispered reply.

"*Muchas gracias,* Leticia." As soon as the *señora* spoke the girl left the room, her face still averted. "There are times when perhaps there is too much submission."

Meredith looked up and thought she caught a twinkle in the old woman's eye.

When Ward returned, they were drinking coffee as Meredith discussed her work in the clinic. He came to her and reached for her hand. She looked up at him with all the love in her heart in her eyes, forgetting, momentarily, that his grandmother was watching. She got to her feet and he pulled her close to him. Snapping black eyes, undimmed by eighty-two years, watched intently as Ward's hand moved up and down her bare arm.

"I will send Leticia for you when the meal is ready," she said to Meredith, dismissing her briskly. "Stay, *nieto,* we have much to talk about."

Ward squeezed Meredith's hand then she went to the door.

"I am an old woman and have not long to wait for a grandson." The words reached Meredith as she left the room and her lips lifted into a grin.

She had quite liked the aristocratic old lady with the bright black eyes who had shown by her every word and look how much she idolized her grandson and wished for his happiness. The interview had gone much better than she had hoped, and there was a lightness to her step when she went up the stairs to the room she would share with Ward.

At the top of the stairs she came to an abrupt halt. A woman stood there glaring at her with the same snapping, black eyes as Ward's grandmother. She was several inches shorter than Meredith and more rounded. Her black hair was parted in the center and drawn severely back into a coil at the nape of her neck. Large, loop earrings swung against her white skin as she tossed her head in an angry gesture. The red slash that was her mouth was set and her eyes spit venom. Meredith almost took a step backward, the woman's hatred was so obvious.

This must be Francisca, she realized, the woman who had nourished the hope of becoming Ward's bride. Meredith almost felt sorry for her. But pity left as soon as the woman spoke.

"You'll never be accepted. A nobody from nowhere! He only married you because he was angry with *Tia* Margarieta for insisting he make our . . . relationship legal in the eyes of the church. Nothing will be changed between us." The words were said with such contempt that a chili crept over Meredith's skin.

"Really?" Anger warmed her.

"I have known Ward since childhood. I was groomed to take my place beside him as his wife." She waved her hands, her eyes fiery.

"Groomed since childhood?" Meredith looked her up and down insolently. "You mean even then no one thought you'd be able to find a husband on your own?"

She stepped around her and went into her room, closed the door, and leaned against it. She was breathless with anger but rather proud that her parting shot had rendered Francisca speechless. It had been a long time since she had traded catty remarks with another woman and the short exchange had left her with pounding temples.

She took deep breaths to calm herself and began to dress for dinner. Ward had told her that his grandmother liked the evening meal to be formal and had suggested she bring her blue chiffon gown.

By the time he came to the room she was calm. Less confident than she had been when she left his grandmother, but calm. She had taken pains with her appearance and knew she looked her best. Ward must have thought so, too. He looked her up and down and smiled.

"Grandmother is not quite so sure I made as disastrous a mistake as she first thought. You must have held your own with her." He took off his shirt and reached for a clean one.

"She's naturally concerned for your happiness. I can't fault her for that."

"You must have convinced her you have my best interests at heart." He grinned at her while his fingers worked at the buttons on his shirt.

"I tried."

She caught the sparkle in his eyes. Happiness engulfed her like a tidal wave and washed Francisca's words from her mind. She was actually beginning to think of herself as his wife, his love. Careful, she cautioned. This was all so new and heady she must not forget that he once ridiculed the "old-fashioned" relationship between one man and one woman.

"Don't let Francisca get under your skin." He was coming toward her with the box containing the diamond earrings and necklace she had worn at the wedding. "She has a boutique in Guadalajara and one in Tulsa and isn't really so bad when you get to know her. She's a damn good businesswoman, and you might as well get used to her."

Meredith went slightly numb on hearing this news, but managed a faint smile. Ward put the necklace around her throat and she lifted her hair so he could fasten the clasp. She took the earrings from his hand and clipped them to her ears.

"Grandmother wore these at her wedding. I want her to see you wearing them."

"Ward, no!" Meredith stood on legs that trembled. "She might resent —"

"No, she won't. She knows we're married. The diamonds were to go to my bride." His mouth curved at one corner. "As far as grandmother is concerned we are married forever. She doesn't believe in divorce."

"I feel as though we're deceiving her." The words came slowly.

"Why?" He raised his brows and somehow his features reminded her of the aristocratic features of his grandmother.

"You know . . . when we talked, we agreed that we might not . . . stay together always." She hated herself for stammering.

His voice was uncompromising, unfriendly. "As a matter of fact, I don't believe in divorce."

Meredith had gone white. "But you said that . . ."

"Are you sorry already, Merry?"

"About what?" She was dumbfounded. Why were they quarreling?

"About marrying me?" He was looking at her as he had the night she arrived at the *hacienda*. He seemed to believe that she was deceiving him in some way.

"No."

Now was not the time to tell him that she was frightened of the responsibility of being his wife, frightened that she was making herself open to heartache because he didn't believe in permanent love between a man and a woman. And terrified that he was having an affair with Francisca. She couldn't tell him any of those things.

I still don't know him, she whispered soundlessly to herself when he turned away from her to go into the adjoining bathroom. How could one love a man yet not know him? And yet it seemed she had known his tall form, the sound of his voice, and the way he moved, forever.

She was standing beside the window looking down into the courtyard when he came back into the room. She heard him rummaging about in his suitcase, then felt his presence beside her.

"It'll take me forever — can you put these in for me?" He held out gold cuff links. All traces of irritation were gone from his face.

He looked darkly handsome in slim-fitting dark pants and a contrasting white jacket, and suddenly she wished to go into his arms, to be held hard against his heart and feel the warm smooth skin of his lean jawline under her fingertips. But she could not make the first move, the fear of rejection was too great. Instead she smiled up at him and with fumbling fingers attached the cuff links.

When she was finished, he framed her face with his hands and the lionlike eyes that looked down into hers held an emotion she was almost sure was tenderness.

"I'd kiss you, but I'd smear your lipstick." How quickly he could change his mood.

"It might be worth it." She forced herself to answer lightly.

He leaned toward her and kissed her very, lightly on the nose.

"It's getting to be a habit," he said with her face still in his hands.

"What is?"

"Wanting to kiss you." He said it lightly, jokingly, and it was hard to keep from communicating all the love she wanted to give him. She covered her confusion with a light laugh and twisted away from him.

They entered the dining room with her hand tucked firmly in the crook of his arm.

They paused and he bent to whisper in her ear. "Eat a lot. Grandma thinks you're too skinny to have babies."

"You're kidding!" Her eyes shone like bright stars until she saw the malice in Francisca's.

The woman was standing beside the se-ñora's chair in a long, flowing dress of red velvet. Its close-fitting bodice had a wide, deep V-neckline that molded her breasts and revealed the pearly whiteness of her neck and shoulders. Her hair was drawn back sleekly and secured to the back of her head. A high, handsome comb, studded with spangles, rose majestically above her head. It was a wholly Spanish look, complete with a long, black, lace handkerchief dangling from her wrist.

All Meredith could think of was how badly she had wanted a red velvet dress when she was a child. She remembered it vividly. She wanted red velvet, longed for red velvet, had asked the Santa Claus at the welfare children's Christmas party for such a dress. She could feel her disappointment, even now, when on Christmas morning she had opened her package to find a pair of green corduroy slacks and a print shirt.

Ward's arm slid around her, possessively, and he urged her toward the two women.

"Darling, I want you to meet Francisca Calderon, a relation of mine."

Meredith forced her stiff lips to smile and nodded to the woman.

"Francisca, my wife, Meredith."

The red lips barely moved. *"Señora."* There was no mistaking the hostility in her eyes.

Ward bent to kiss his grandmother's cheek and on impulse Meredith did the same. The old lady looked long and hard at her before she smiled. "The necklace becomes you. Did Ward tell you I wore it on my wedding day?"

"Yes, he did, *señora.* And I was proud to wear it on mine."

Ward helped his grandmother to her feet and handed her a silver-handled cane. Meredith was surprised when she stood to see how small she was. She had never considered herself tall, but she towered over these two women as much as Ward towered over her.

The rectangular table had been laid for four in intimate proximity at one end of the polished wood. The setting breathed of quiet elegance, from the candles to the vivid poinsettia blooms floating in a delicate glass bowl. The *señora* moved to the left of the table with Francisca beside her. Ward

178

seated his grandmother and politely held out the chair for Francisca before coming around to seat Meredith. He sat at the head of the table as if he were the master of this large estate.

It was not as difficult a meal to get through as Meredith had anticipated. Ward made sure she was included in the conversation and as time went on and Francisca remained silent it became easier.

The meal was superbly cooked and served and ended with a delicious creme caramel dessert. Openly admitting to having a sweet tooth, Meredith devoured every spoonful, much to Saldana's delight.

The *señora* left them as soon as the meal was finished. Ward walked her to her room with Saldana trotting along behind. Meredith, not wanting to remain alone with Francisca, walked out into the large entrance hall. She hesitated for only a moment before she went up the stairs.

She glanced at her watch after she closed the door to the bedroom. Perhaps she shouldn't have disappeared after Ward and his grandmother left them. Francisca might think she was avoiding her. Well, in fact, she was, but not because she felt intimidated. She was confident she could hold her own with the fiery Mexican woman. It was just that conflict was upsetting to her and she wanted to keep that happy, peaceful glow that had been with her since her wedding night. In a few minutes she would return to the sitting room.

Her honeymoon was almost over. Tomorrow they would go back to the *hacienda* and perhaps by the end of the week to Tulsa. She had almost succeeded in banishing the doubt that she was incapable of filling the position demanded of Ward's wife. The last four days had been the most wonderful days of her life and anything that could happen to her in the future would pale in comparison.

She stood beside the window and looked down on the courtyard. It was dark, but lights from the room below cast a soft glow on the statue of the Madonna standing peacefully in the garden. Meredith was about to turn away when she heard Ward's voice. She looked for him, then realized he was on the veranda beneath the window.

"That's nonsense, Francisca." His voice was biting in the way it could be when he was out of patience.

"But why did you do it, Ward? Why did you marry that . . . ?"

"I don't have to justify my actions to you. I never gave you any reason to believe I'd marry you."

"But I have to know." The voice was soft and persistent. There was a pause during which Ward didn't say anything. "She's in love with you. You only have to look at her to know that!" The words were bitter. "Are you in love with her, *querido?*"

Meredith's face grew warm and she tilted her head toward the window, anxious to hear Ward's answer.

There was the briefest of hesitations, then, "That need not concern you. Our relationship has not changed, Francisca. Meredith will not interfere."

Meredith clutched her throat. She wanted to tear herself away from the window, away from the words that could spell ruin to her newly found happiness. But fear and hunger for the truth, no matter how destructive, kept her prisoner beside the window.

"I don't want *her* to know." Francisca had a sob in her voice.

"She won't know unless you or Luis tell her. I don't know what you're worrying about. I'll take care of you. You know that."

"I know that, *querido.* But I thought it would be as your wife. *Tia* Margarieta wanted —"

"Enough, Francisca! I'm not a boy to be commanded to wed." A soft shuddering sob by the woman below reflected Meredith's own feelings. "Go to bed, *prima mía*. Tomorrow you will go back to Guadalajara with us. I have a meeting at the plant and then you and I will go to the boutique. How's that?"

"I don't have much choice, do I?"

"No, you don't. It's up to you to adjust to this new situation."

"I hate her!" This was hissed with fiery venom.

Ward laughed. "Well, I don't."

"Tell me you don't love her?"

Softly and patiently Ward said, "Francisca, I don't think that need concern us . . ."

The words trailed away. They were moving into the house.

The word "us" echoed in Meredith's brain, causing her limbs to come trembling back to life. White-faced and sick at heart, she turned and went to the bathroom. There, the door locked behind her, safe from Ward's eyes if he should come to their room, she took great sobbing breaths while she fought for control. No longer a barely tolerated visitor in someone's house, for the first time in her life she had begun to feel that she was wanted, that she belonged. Was it all going to be taken from her so soon? she thought miserably. Or were her own fears of rejection making her jump to conclusions?

Choking back the sobs, Meredith vowed that she would keep her suspicions to herself. A confrontation would only let Ward know how much she loved him, how utterly she was in his power. She couldn't do it — she had been hurt too many times before. The tears spilled out from her anguished eyes and her mouth worked convulsively. So much for no secrets between them, she thought bitterly. Very slowly control won and she opened tightly clenched hands and pressed them to the cold marble washbasin.

This was all her own damn fault! She had wanted so desperately to believe that he would come to love her as she loved him. Now she feared that he never intended to be a faithful husband. She stared at her white face in the mirror. You are a gullible, dumb . . . broad, Meredith Moore! Tell him to bug off, you don't need him. Her eyes filled again. What if she was wrong? Either way, she couldn't let him go.

She went back into the bedroom, took off the chiffon dress and flung it over a chair, removed the earrings and necklace, grabbed up a nightgown, and was back in the bathroom in a matter of seconds. With trembling hands she washed her face. Taking the wet cloth with her, she returned to the bedroom and climbed into the massive bed.

A minute later Ward came into the room. She was curled up on the far side of the bed, the wet cloth over her eyes.

"What's the matter, Merry?" He sat down beside her. "Do you have a headache?"

She nodded and gave a soft groan and wished with all her heart that was all that was the matter with her.

"Did it just come on?"

Again she nodded and pressed her hands to her temples. She wanted to scream *liar!* Instead she gritted her teeth and whispered almost inaudibly, "Let me sleep. I'll be all right in the morning."

"Sure. Go to sleep." His hand lingered on her upper bare arm. The bed swayed slightly when his weight was removed from it.

Meredith huddled, miserable, on the bed. She could hear him moving about and opened her eyes a crack. He was hanging her dress in the zippered bag they had used to bring it and her other things from the plane. He put the earrings and necklace back into their box and tucked it into her suitcase. When he began to remove his clothes she closed her eyes.

Ward got into the bed, moved close up against her back and put his arms around her. She felt his kiss on her shoulder before he settled back and was almost instantly asleep, his breathing coming gently against her neck. No longer needing the cloth to hide her swollen eyes, she removed it and let the tears slide down her cheeks. . . .

It was the muffled sound of Ward moving about the room, trying not to wake her while he dressed, that awakened her. For a few seconds she lay motionless, then memory returned, and with it, pain. She pretended sleep until he left the room, then threw back the covers and sat up. This morning she was firmly in control of her emotions, determined to play out the charade.

She managed to put on a good face when she said goodbye to the *señora.* The very nature of the occasion demanded it. If her voice stuck in her throat, it was due to the very real headache that last night's emotional upheaval had left with her.

Francisca was in better, if not exuberant, spirits as she stood in the foyer beside her cases. Ward had not mentioned the fact that she was going back to Guadalajara with them and Meredith had ignored her.

Meredith dreaded being with them in the close quarters of the plane, but it was easier than she expected. Ward spent most of the time in the cockpit talking with the pilot, leaving the two women to sit alone. Meredith felt no obligation to make small talk, and the silence pressed down upon her like a tangible thing. The monotonous drone of the engines soon lulled her into a feverish daydream where her fears were given free rein. What was she supposed to say to Francisca, her husband's mistress? That she could have him on weekends but he was hers on weekdays and holidays? Half asleep now, Meredith thought miserably that somehow she must find a way to end this charade, this mockery of a marriage, before she was irretrievably hurt.

Chapter Eleven

When they arrived at the *hacienda* in Chapala, they were greeted with the news that Norma Sanderson, Ward's stepmother, had returned. Ward reacted with a grimace, Francisca with a smile, and Meredith with the desire to retreat to her room as soon as possible. Ward foiled her escape by attaching his fingers firmly to her wrist.

"No use putting off the inevitable. All the best generals agree it's better to attack than to be attacked." She sensed his amusement and she grew more annoyed. He started off down the hall taking her with him.

Ward opened the door to the sitting room and walked in as if he knew his stepmother would be there, and she was. She sat in regal splendor behind a magnificent silver service as if she were posed for a photograph. She looked even more haughty and aristocratic than Meredith had expected, although younger and more beautiful. She was slender, and blond, and Meredith instinctively knew she was tall even though she remained seated and looked at her with cold, blue eyes. She had exceedingly lovely, almost wrinkle-free skin and held her head in the slightly tilted position that women use when they want the skin of their neck to appear firm. It was obvious she was aware of the marriage, disapproved, and had chosen to show her displeasure by refusing to greet them when they arrived, forcing them to come to her.

Her coldness and hostility didn't seem to bother Ward.

"Hello, Norma. Back so soon? Wasn't there any royalty aboard the cruise ship? I thought you'd have caught an earl or a count by now and be ensconced in a castle playing queen over the peons."

"Don't be vulgar," she snapped.

He laughed. "Well, if you didn't find a mate, I did. This is my wife, Meredith." He placed an arm across Meredith's shoulders, and his hand caressed the side of her face possessively, his eyes full of sparkling enjoyment.

Meredith smiled pleasantly, but her thoughts were racing. She was only an instrument of his spite! Not only was he rebelling against his grandmother's wishes when he'd married her, but he'd done it to spite his stepmother, as well.

"Darling." He was smiling down into her eyes. "This is my sweet-tempered step-mother, Norma."

The woman didn't even glance at Meredith. Her eyes were focused on Ward with pure hatred.

"This," she tilted her head in Meredith's direction, "I would have suspected of you, Ward. But I did not expect you to take advantage of my absence to persuade Cullen to leave. If anything happens to him, it will be on your conscience and I'll never forgive you as long as I live."

Meredith gave a start at the news, but Ward coolly controlled his surprise.

"That's the best news I've heard in a long time. Where's he going?"

"Not going. Gone. It seems he received a telephone call from the girl, the one that hung around here for so long after the accident. She's the sister of that brassy woman Jim married. He packed that ridiculous van, took Antonio, and left without a word to anyone. It isn't like Cullen to be so thought-less. You must have instigated his leaving. Heaven knows where he is. He hasn't called and I'm worried sick."

"Oh, I'm so glad!" The words burst from Meredith. "Not that you're worried, Mrs. Sanderson, but that Cullen and Becky will have a chance to be together and work out their problems. I know he loves her."

The eyes the woman turned on Meredith were filled with cold contempt. "You know nothing of the sort. Kindly keep out of this. This is family business."

"Hold it, Norma!" Ward's words were sharp. "Merry is my wife and I expect her to be treated like family."

"Family? You're a fine one to be talking about family."

"Yes, family. And I'm thinking you had better be remembering who is the head of this one. Speaking of family, where is Maggie?"

Meredith moved away from Ward's encircling arm. She began to grow hot and angry, tension like acid in her stomach. She had to get out of this room. The dissension here was straining her nerves to the breaking point.

"Sophia took Maggie to Carmen's," Norma said. "I couldn't bear the sight of her moping about the house."

Ward urged Meredith toward a chair and pressed her down into it. "Pour the coffee, Norma. I could use some and so could Merry." While he was speaking the telephone rang, then stopped when it was answered in another part of the house.

He brought coffee to Meredith and was about to sit down with his own when one of the servants beckoned to him. He went to the doorway and they talked in low tones. He returned and set his cup on the table.

"Excuse me. I have a call."

"If it's Cullen, tell him I want to talk to him."

"It isn't Cullen."

Silence fell when Ward left the room. Norma turned contemptuous eyes on Meredith and left them there. The stare was meant to put her firmly in the category headed "inferior." The knowledge made Meredith coldly angry and she returned the stare with equal arrogance.

"You didn't lose much time, did you?"

Meredith refused to answer or change her expression. She had learned, long ago, that to say nothing was sometimes more effective than saying a lot.

"You had to have a better game plan than just getting him to bed. Ward's been to bed with scores of women."

Meredith saw with satisfaction that her psychology was working. Norma's cheeks were now tinged with color. She decided to wait a moment longer before speaking.

"One can't help but wonder how you managed."

"Wonder all you like." Meredith gave her a sly smile.

"The Sandersons are among the best-known and most respected families in the southwest. We are also wealthy, as I'm sure you knew when you came here. With wealth goes the responsibility to retain . . . certain values." Her eyes were bitingly sharp and Meredith had to admire her control. She was furiously angry. "I simply don't understand Ward besmirching himself and . . . all of us, in this manner."

"Shouldn't you be discussing this with him?" Meredith asked coolly.

Norma ignored the question and asked one of her own. "Who are you?" She spoke with a ponderous solemnity and Meredith was forced to swallow an almost hysterical giggle.

"I'm Meredith Moore. Meredith Sanderson, now," she corrected. "I'm twenty-five years old, I'm an x-ray technician, my parents are dead, and I've got all my own teeth." She showed them, her smile barbed. Norma gazed at her, her face set in hard, angry lines.

Ward came in and picked up his coffee. He remained standing. Meredith got to her feet, smiling pleasantly, proud she was able to do so when she really wanted to walk over and punch this priggish woman in the mouth. She would have to think of a special torture for Ward for what he had done to her, for using her to get at Norma.

"It was lovely meeting you, Mrs. Sanderson," she said with exaggerated sweetness. "If you'll excuse me, I'll go up and unpack." She stood for a moment looking from one to the other. Neither spoke or looked at her and she allowed her face to show all the scorn she was feeling for them. Ward looked up and she met his eyes. They stared at each other for a long moment, blue eyes contemptuous, tawny ones filled with anger.

Meredith walked away from them and out into the hallway where she paused to compose herself before making the long trek up the stairway. Norma's voice reached her easily.

"How could you do such a thing to us? Why did you marry a creature like that? She is ill-bred, has the manners of a barmaid, and is entirely out of our class. Your grandmother and I would have been happy to accept Francisca into the family. If not her, then some other girl from a good family. You did this to spite me, didn't you, Ward? You've never liked me from the day your father brought me home. You'd do anything to make me suffer. Even this!"

"Shut up, Norma!" The shout echoed into the empty hall. "And as long as you've brought it up . . . no, I've never liked you from the moment my father brought you home. You cared nothing for him. You cared for his money and his position. You have never cared for anything in your life except yourself and Cullen, and your grasping hands have almost squeezed the life out of him. My responsibility to you, my dear step-mother, is to see that you are cared for in the style you've grown accustomed to and that is all. Kindly keep your nose out of my affairs!"

"You'll not drag Cullen down with you. I won't have it!"

Meredith fled up the stairs and into her room. The quarrel going on downstairs brought back memories of how she used to cringe under the bedcovers when her foster parents quarreled. How she hated conflict! She was glad she had the unpacking to occupy her mind, but it didn't last nearly long enough.

When her suitcases were stored in the back of the wardrobe, she picked up the ornate wooden box holding the earrings and necklace. She couldn't resist opening the box and looking at them. They were so beautiful, but not for her. She snapped the box shut and placed it on the stand beside the bed.

With nothing to do she paced the room, stood beside the window, and looked down on the courtyard. Her nerves were strung as tight as a bow-string. She would take a bath. Almost always she could relax in a warm bath.

Even then, her thoughts refused to lie still. She seemed to be pressed to make a decision and she finally came to forming a plan. She would not mention to Ward until they reached Tulsa that she now felt their marriage was a mistake and that she wished to terminate it. Somehow she couldn't bear to think of all the pleasure her decision would bring to Norma and Francisca. She didn't want to embarrass Ward, either. She had to admit he had placed his cards firmly on the table when he asked her to marry him. He had made it clear he didn't believe in that old-fashioned relationship between one man and one woman. But he had promised to be a faithful husband! It wasn't his fault she had fallen in love with him, she reasoned. She had been lulled into a mythical world during that wonderful honeymoon. The nights they had lain in each other's arms had been heavenly. Ward had thought so too. He had said so repeatedly.

Meredith knew, despite her surface bravado, that when she was under stress all her old insecurities came rising to the surface. Could they be blinding her now? If only she hadn't overheard that conversation with Francisca. Even now, the remembered words cut into her heart like a knife.

She was dressed and sitting beside the window when Ward came into the room. It had been several hours since she left him. Had he been with his stepmother or Francisca all this time? Meredith longed to throw herself into his arms, to confess her fears and suspicions, but he was looking at her like a stranger, his face turned to ice. He stood with his back to the door and spoke expressionlessly.

"There's someone downstairs to see you."

"To see me?" She thought he must be joking, but he wasn't smiling. "Cullen is back!" She got to her feet.

"Not Cullen. It's Crowley. Dr. Paul Crowley."

The nail file fluttered from her nervous fingers and for a moment she was speechless.

"Paul? Here? I can't believe it!"

"Well, it's true. And if you don't want him

brainwashed, you'd better go on down. Norma took him in hand as soon as I left him." He was so quiet she didn't know if he was angry or indifferent. Coherent thoughts fled her mind. She was shocked into numbness.

"What does he want?" she asked through stiff lips.

"How in the hell do I know?" He shoved himself away from the door. "He called from the airport and Ramon called me to the phone. He said he had business with you."

"Was that the call you took while . . ."

"Yes."

"Why didn't you tell me he was coming instead of waiting until he arrived?" She was resentful and didn't care if he knew it. She glared at him and his face changed to weariness.

"I wanted time to think. Go on down and see what he wants." She went to the door, but his next words stopped her. "He came about a week late, didn't he?"

She turned to look at him, opened her mouth to say something, thought better of it, and went out the door. Her mind was spinning wildly. What in the world was Paul doing here? And how did he know where to find her? Then she remembered. Maude, of course. Paul had met Maude on one occasion and she was completely charmed by him as most women were. It was too bad, she thought angrily, that she hadn't filled Maude in on just what a conniver he was.

Norma's tinkling laughter and Paul's deeper tones guided her to the library. She stood in the doorway and watched them. Paul's head was bent attentively to Norma. He certainly was a beautiful man. His blond hair, thick and shining, was styled to cover the tops of his ears. A deep tan from the health club's sunlamps enhanced his features, which had the classic lines of a Greek god. When he smiled, deep dents appeared in his cheeks and his lips spread to reveal teeth worthy of a toothpaste commercial. He was tall, slender, and always dressed right for the occasion. She saw him now with new eyes. He was a beautiful doll. Nothing more. How could she have devoted four years of her life to this shallow, conceited man?

He saw her. "Meredith. How nice it is to see you again."

"Hello, Paul."

"I'll leave you to conduct your . . . business, doctor. My invitation for dinner and to spend the night stands if you should change your mind."

Paul took Norma's hand and raised it to his lips. "Thank you, gracious lady. As much as I would like to enjoy your hospitality, I have friends waiting for me in Guadalajara and an important operation to perform tomorrow."

Meredith raised her eyes to the ceiling. Shades of Doctor Kildare! This was Paul at his best and, from the look on Norma's face, she was swallowing it hook, line, and sinker. He walked the beaming woman to the door and when she passed through it he closed it behind her and turned to face Meredith. The smile was gone, now, and in its place was, of all things, concern.

"Why did you run away, my darling? You knew the thing with Connie wouldn't last." He came to her and took her hand before she could step away from him. "You're not still angry with me? I've missed you! I didn't realize how much you meant to me until you left me."

Meredith jerked her hand from his and moved a few feet away from him.

"I'm not angry, Paul. I'm through with you. Finished."

"Darling, you can't be. We can't be finished after all we've been to each other." There was soft pleading in his voice and Meredith had the hysterical desire to laugh.

"Stop it! I know all your acts. I'm married now, but I'm sure you knew that when you came here."

"I did know that and I also know that you love me, as I love you."

"Love me? You don't love anyone but yourself, Paul." This time a chuckle escaped her.

He was quiet for a long moment. Then suddenly his hand darted out and seized her wrist, tightening until she gasped with pain and indignation.

"Don't laugh at me," he snapped.

"Let go." She tugged at her wrist.

"Stand still." Paul's face was petulant and vicious.

She raised angry eyes to his. All the loathing and contempt she felt for him was mirrored in her face. "Get out! Get out before I call my husband and have you thrown out!"

He threw her hand from him and turned his back to her. When he faced her again, his look was unruffled and arrogant.

"How did you ever get that cold fish to marry you?" No pretense, now. The charm had gone with her rejection of him.

"What do you want, Paul? Say it and go."

"I'll have to admit you're smarter than I gave you credit for." He spoke as if she hadn't said anything. "He married you and you should be able to get a hefty divorce settlement. Face it, darling. There will be a divorce. You don't have the polish to hack this sort of life. His mother as much as told me the family was devastated because of the marriage."

"His stepmother," she corrected firmly. "How did you find me?" She knew, but wanted him to say it.

"Maude Fiske. Who else? She also came through with the news you had married Tulsa's favorite son. Well, maybe not the favorite, but certainly one of the richest."

"Is that why you're here? You thought to go through me to get to Ward's money?" There was a sneering edge in her voice. "Did Connie let you down, or was it her father?"

"Forget Connie. And of course I came to get money. You owe me, you know. After all, I did contribute to our *joint* income. I want what you have in the savings account." His mouth twisted cruelly.

She was shocked almost speechless. This was the last thing she would have expected of him. "You didn't save one cent of what I have in the savings account and you know it. That little amount of money would be a drop in the bucket to you."

"Every little bit helps, darling."

"You're not . . . serious!"

"Oh, but I am. I want it. I'm going to open a practice in Minneapolis."

"So? What does that have to do with me?"

"Stop hedging. I want the money. I need it."

She knew he was lying. The amount of money she had wouldn't buy reception-room furniture for any office he would open. He had to make her suffer in order to restore his hurt vanity and injured pride.

"And if I don't give it to you?" She met his eyes levelly.

"Then I shall accept Mrs. Sanderson's invitation to spend the week. And as a doctor and someone from your . . . past, I will feel it is my obligation to warn the family that you are a nymphomaniac and were discharged from the clinic for molesting the male patients." He looked into her shocked eyes and smiled. A part of his crushed ego was restored. "You know I can be very persuasive when I set my mind to it."

"Ward wouldn't believe you!"

"It doesn't matter if he were to believe me or not. His mother would. She would spread it among his friends. The people in Tulsa would believe it. You'd be blackballed! Ward Sanderson and his bride would be on every scandal sheet in the country. He'll wish he'd never set eyes on you."

"I never, in my wildest dreams, thought you were this vile, this corrupt."

"Now you know. But don't start with the 'after all I've done for you' routine. You were paid tenfold for what you did for me. I'm not stupid. You had a certain amount of prestige because I paid attention to you. Now are you going to get me the money or shall I join my hostess?"

Meredith was shaken, heartsick; not because of his words but because she had been such a gullible, blind fool. Suddenly tiredness welled up in her, enveloping her like a shroud. She felt as if her head were bursting. Hate and frustration joggled against despair.

"I'll get my purse and give you a check," she said wearily, hearing the defeat in her own voice.

She left him on trembling legs and during the long trek up the stairs prayed that Ward wouldn't be in the bedroom when she reached it. She couldn't face him, or anyone else, at this moment. He wasn't there and she grabbed up her purse and left the room in a matter of seconds.

Paul was standing pretty much as she had left him. She walked past him without looking at him and sat down at the desk. He came to look over her shoulder and took the checkbook from her hand and thumbed through it.

"The last time I looked at this you had considerably more on deposit. What did you do with it?"

"I spent it on airfare. Take it and get out. I hope I never have to see you again." From somewhere inside her hate and fury hardened her voice.

"You'll see me again. Never doubt that." He put the check in his pocket. His fingertips caressed the polished wood of the desk and his eyes lingered on the rich draperies and the priceless Persian carpet. "Tulsa is looking better to me all the time. I never did like the winters in Minneapolis."

"Get out of my life and stay out!" Meredith was screaming inside, but her voice was low, controlled.

Paul laughed. "Stay married to your sugar daddy for as long as you can, sweetie. I'll expect regular donations, to my . . . free-will clinic."

She clenched her fists and held them tightly to her sides to keep them from flying up and hitting him.

"You won't get another cent from me."

"Not you, darling. Your husband, Ward

Sanderson. Play your cards right and he can make us both happy. Hang in there, now, and I'll see you soon."

He opened the door and stepped out into the hall. Meredith followed and her stricken eyes saw Ward coming toward them. Paul, charming once again, moved forward and held out his hand.

"It was nice meeting you, Sanderson. Thanks for lending me your wife. She's been very helpful . . . beyond my expectations, as a matter of fact. You've got yourself a real little jewel here. She's not only beautiful, but smart too."

Ward took the hand extended to him and nodded his head briefly, his eyes resting intently on Meredith's white face. "You're leaving." He said it bluntly.

"I must. A doctor's time isn't his own." He looked fondly at Meredith. "Goodbye. Meredith. I sincerely wish you all the happiness you deserve."

"Goodbye." She thought her face would crack when her lips moved. She didn't dare look at Ward. She kept her eyes focused on Paul, all the while despising herself for ever having thought he was a decent human being.

Paul went down the hall and Ward followed to see him out. Meredith stood clutching the door frame until they were out of sight, then with a moan of pain she ran up the stairs, wishing with all her heart she could turn back the clock and relive the last forty-eight hours. In a trancelike state she closed the door and rested against the paneling, too stricken to be aware of her surroundings. She took deep breaths and awareness came rushing back. Ward would want some answers. She had to think. She went to the bathroom and bathed her face with a wet cloth, re-touched her make-up and returned to the bedroom to see Ward coming in the door, her purse in his hand.

"You left this on the desk."

"Thank you." She took the purse from him, placed it on the bureau, and picked up her hairbrush.

"Meredith!"

The voice was loud, harsh, and cut across the room like a whip. She jumped as if he had struck her. When she turned, she caught him looking at her in a way that shriveled her soul. It was a cold, angry, violent look, like the time he had accused her of flirting in Acapulco, only a hundred times worse. She stared at him silently.

"Were you so upset to see him go that you couldn't see him to the door?" His eyes trapped hers. Her heart beat so fast it seemed to fill her ears.

"I was glad to see him go. I never want to see him again."

"Don't lie. Your expression was transparent." He stood there, his feet spread apart, his arms across his chest, for what felt like an eon. She stared back with wide, sorrowful eyes. "I didn't like him," Ward said slowly. "He's a phoney if I ever saw one." There was something strange in his voice. Accusation? He came close to her and her eyes were level with his chin. He needs to shave again, she thought crazily.

"What do you want me to say? I didn't ask him to come here." Her heart was pounding. She tried to think empty thoughts. She didn't want him to read anything in them. She didn't want him to know how . . . frightened she was.

"What did he want, Merry?" There was gentleness in his tone, now, and she wanted to cry.

"He wanted information." She didn't look at him. She knew that he knew she was lying.

"And you carry that information around in your purse. I'm no fool! If you don't want to tell me, say so, but don't lie!" His words were measured.

Suddenly she was tired of it all. Exhausted. Tired of being pushed by Paul, by Norma, by Francisca, by . . . him! She felt as if someone had stuck a knife in her and was slowly twisting it.

"I don't want to tell you!" The words burst from her angrily.

An interminable silence filled the room. She knew that the fragile hope she had secretly nourished that perhaps he might give up Francisca and come to love her had just vanished.

"That's better. At least we're being honest." That couldn't be hurt in his voice. She glanced up to see a nerve pulsing beside his eye.

Wearily she turned from him. She wanted to go home. Home? Where was that? Her eyes filled with tears and overflowed down on her cheeks.

"Do you mind if I lie down for a while?"

"Go ahead. I won't stop you."

The door closed behind him and she was alone. It was a relief and a sickening misery in one. She could cry now. There was no one to see her. She lay down on the bed. The tears came in an overwhelming flood. They poured from her eyes, rolled down her cheeks, and seeped between her fingers that were pressed hard against her face. Presently she roused herself long enough to take off her shoes and slip between the sheets. Her mind longed for rest and she sought the sweet oblivion of sleep.

She awakened during the night and lay staring into the darkness. She was alone. How strange, she mused, that after sleeping beside Ward for such a short time she could feel so alone without him beside her, without waking to find her head pillowed on his shoulder, his hand cupping her breast.

It had not taken him long to return to his old love, she thought bitterly, and tears once again began to slide down her cheeks. Throughout the night she tossed restlessly, wondering what would have happened to her if she had not left Minnesota. Would she have kept reliving the pain of Paul's rejection? No! She liked to think she had more sense than that.

She must have slept because when she woke there was something warm and soft beside her. Her eyes flew open and she stared into Maggie's pixie face.

"Hi."

"Did I wake you up?"

"Yes, but it's all right."

"Can I stay for a while?"

"Sure, if you want too."

Maggie moved nearer, slid an arm around

her neck, and snuggled into the curve of her body. Meredith hugged her tightly, seeking to comfort and be comforted.

They were lying like that when Sophia came looking for Maggie. "There you are, little mule. You no bother the *señora. Señor* Ward say let her sleep."

"She's no bother, Sophia. Do you think she and I could have our breakfast here in the room?"

"Ah . . . *si*." A smile appeared. "Get dressed, little mule. I bring breakfast."

"Sophia," Meredith called as she opened the door. "*Señor* Ward? Is he . . ."

"Guadalajara, *señora.* He take the *señorita* with him."

Thank God. Meredith wasn't sure if she had said the words aloud or not. She was relieved she wouldn't have to face Ward or Francisca for hours. Maybe not until evening. It would give her some time to get herself together.

She devoted the day to Maggie. They played games, rearranged the furniture in the dollhouse, dressed all the dolls, and read stories. Meredith read dozens of stories, mimicking voices when possible to keep the child amused.

In the middle of the afternoon, when Maggie's head had fallen against her shoulder, Meredith eased the child down on to the thick carpet and placed a pillow beneath her head. She no longer had an excuse to stay in the room, but was reluctant to leave it so she placed all the toys in their proper places and stacked the books back in the bookshelves.

Sophia came silently into the room. *"Señora."* Her face was unsmiling for once. "Come to the telephone. *Señor* Cullen wish to speak to you."

Meredith's smile was real. "Cullen?"

"Señora," Sophia's voice was urgent. "He no want to speak to his *madre.*"

"He wants to speak to me and not his mother?"

"Ramon say you come. Come to *Señor* Ward's telephone."

Meredith followed her down the hall into a large square room. It was a man's room, furnished with large pieces of heavy, dark furniture. There were no extra accessories. Everything was functional and necessary. The telephone was on a table beside the bed and the receiver was off the hook. Meredith picked it up.

"Hello, Cullen?"

"Merry, Merry, my marshmallow Merry. How are you?" He was happy. There was a joyous tremor in his voice.

"I'm fine." She wasn't, but she hoped she convinced him she was. "Where are you?"

"I'm with Becky. We're going to be married and I'm going to write music and she's going to raise horses and kids!"

"Cullen! How wonderful!"

"I got to thinking about you and big brother, marshmallow. You've done miracles with old sober-sides. And Becky, well, she decided to call me after Ruth got back from the wedding. I've been a stupid ass, Merry. I sat there feeling sorry for myself, thinking my life was over, and hell, the best part is yet to come."

"Give my love to Becky and tell her I think she's the luckiest girl in the world."

"Didn't you mean second luckiest, marshmallow?" Cullen laughed and waited, but she could think of nothing to say. "Ramon said Ward was at the plant. Tell him where I am, will you?"

He hadn't mentioned his mother and she felt she should tell him she was here. "Cullen? Your mother is here. She's terribly worried about you."

There was a short silence before he spoke. "Yes, I know. She wired she was coming. That's when I decided to split. Couldn't face up to it. I was going to wait until you and Ward came back because I hated to leave Maggie, but if I'd stayed there would have been a battle royal. Just say I'm a coward." He laughed. "How is the little monster?"

"She misses you. She loves you very much."

"I miss her. Do you suppose she could spend some time with me and Becky?" There was an anxious tone to his voice.

"I'm sure she can. Of course I can't speak for Ward, but I'm . . . sure she can." She repeated herself because of the sudden lump in her throat and it was something safe to say.

"Is everything okay, Merry?"

"Everything's fine, Cullen. We had a wonderful time in Acapulco. We stayed at that fabulous hotel where Howard Hughes stayed and we saw the divers dive off the cliffs. There were people there from all over the world. Flowers were everywhere. The water was warm and we found a spot on the beach that wasn't overloaded with people. And, oh yes . . . I met Ward's grandmother. She was naturally concerned about our marriage, but she was very gracious and I liked her." Oh, why don't I shut up, she thought desperately. "Cullen . . ."

"Did you meet Francisca, Merry?"

She drew in a deep breath. "Yes. Yes, I

did. She came back here with us. I think she . . . went with Ward today."

"Damn!"

"It's all right, Cullen." She forced a laugh.

"If she and my mother make it rough for you, Merry, tell Ward. He'll set them straight."

Meredith wanted to say, "A lot you know, my lad." Instead she said, "It's okay, Cullen. We'll be going to Tulsa soon."

"Hang tough, marshmallow. You've got me and Ward on your side. Say . . . take down this number and have him call me."

Meredith copied the number and repeated it to him to make sure it was correct. Then after wishing him and Becky happiness she hung up and wrote a message to Ward beneath the number.

The afternoon rolled into evening. Meredith wished for Ward's return and dreaded it. She bathed, shampooed her hair, and put on her cream silk dress. Somehow she didn't want to wear the new clothes Ward had bought for her. She knew she would have to get over the feeling if they stayed here at the *hacienda* much longer. The things she had brought with her were beginning to look worn.

As time for the evening meal approached, her anxiety grew. Would she be expected to take the meal with Mrs. Sanderson if Ward and Francisca didn't return? She stood beside the window and watched car lights approach the *hacienda.* A cold stillness enveloped her as she watched. The car stopped and Luis and Francisca got out. Where was Ward? Was he going to stay at his apartment in town? At least he wasn't with Francisca, she thought with a certain malicious satisfaction.

Her legs were trembly and her heart was beating too fast. She realized this weakness was partly due to the fact she hadn't eaten anything since her light breakfast. If Ward didn't return, there would be no reason for her to go to the dining room.

Sophia brought her a tray and she ate hungrily. She felt some disgust with herself for being so cowardly. Next time, she promised the braver part of herself, next time she'd put on her best face and defy them, but not tonight.

She sat beside the window until almost midnight before she put on her gown and robe. With slow, tired movements she cleaned her face and brushed her teeth and returned to her vigil.

Once again automobile lights came up the drive. This time Ward got out of the car and stood for a moment in the courtyard.

Meredith didn't know for sure if he looked toward the window, but she drew back and groped her way to the bed and lay there trembling.

Chapter Twelve

Tension laid a grip on Meredith, making her oblivious to all but the fear that Ward would come to her room and expect to make love to her. She couldn't let him! She couldn't . . . now that she knew about Francisca. It was too much to expect of her. Even if she still loved him, she couldn't do it! Though she could be worrying for nothing, she reasoned with herself. He hadn't come to her last night. There was the possibility that he had already become weary of her and had begun the gradual easing out of their relationship.

Imprisoned in her thoughts, she scarcely heard the door open. The lights were switched on, blinding her momentarily. She sat up, clutching the bedclothes to her. Ward closed the door and came to stand in the middle of the room. He was wearing dark slacks and a white shift. His tie was loosened and several buttons on his shirt were open, yet there was nothing relaxed about his attitude or his expression. His face was completely colorless and the small pulse beside his eye was throbbing in a way she had seen before when he was upset.

She half rose to get out of bed, but his eyes passed over her coldly and then away. She sank back down. "Cullen called. He wants you to call him. I left the number on the pad beside your telephone."

Silence.

He took a step toward her. His shoulders were slumped tiredly and his limp more pronounced than she had ever noticed before. Watching him, she marveled that a man who looked so weary and pale could grow even more so before her eyes. Now she was terrified and wasn't sure why. She drew in a deep, quivering breath.

"What is it, Ward?" When he didn't answer, fear burgeoned inside her and she dug her nails into her palms and tried to think what dreadful news could make him look like this. The silence went on and she couldn't stand it. "What is it? What's happened?"

He was close to the bed now, staring down at her as if he despised her. Why in the world was he acting like this?

"I waited up for you tonight," she said because she had to say something.

It seemed as if he hadn't even heard her. "Something very unpleasant has happened.

The diamond earrings are missing." The words came out of the frozen mask that was his face. "Would you have any idea where they might be?"

"The . . . earrings?" The words hung in the air. "I . . . don't know." She looked at the table where she had placed the box when she took it from her suitcase the day before. It wasn't there. "Didn't you put them away? I don't have them."

"I *know* you don't have them. Until this afternoon Paul Crowley had them." His words were slow, measured. "There's got to be some logical explanation." And he waited for Meredith's reply.

"What are you talking about? That's impossible!" Meredith felt as if she were falling into a bottomless pit. Ward would naturally be extremely upset over the stolen diamonds, but she could not fathom why he was staring at her coldly, his eyes angry and guarded. He remained silent, waiting for her to speak.

Suddenly it dawned on her — he suspected her! The realization crushed her like a living force. It was a nightmare, of course. This couldn't be happening to her. Did Ward actually expect her to defend herself? She crossed her arms over her chest and stared defiantly back at him.

Wearily, Ward put his hand in his pocket, drew it out and held it palm up. The earrings lay in his palm. From his other pocket he brought out a folded sheet of paper.

"Dr. Crowley apparently got cold feet. He returned the diamonds."

She shook her head numbly, too shocked to speak.

"They were delivered to my office this afternoon by special courier along with this letter. Read it for yourself." He tossed it down, but didn't move away.

Sitting on the side of the bed, her bare feet on the floor, she unfolded the paper with trembling fingers, and began to read. "Dear Mr. Sanderson: No doubt you will be surprised to find enclosed your wedding gift to your bride. Had I realized the value of the earrings, I would not have accepted them when Meredith insisted that I take them to help finance the opening of my clinic. I am sure she has, by now, informed you about our former relationship and that I came to your home to collect funds from our joint bank account. This is true. When she left Rochester, she took everything and, as I'm sure you can understand, I wanted what was mine. Meredith gave me a check for a very small portion of what was in the account. I wish her no harm, but in all honesty I cannot accept the earrings. I am returning them to you for safe keeping. I sincerely hope that your relationship with Meredith will not be concluded as mine was, with possessiveness and jealousy threatening my career. Dr. Paul Crowley."

The paper fluttered from Meredith's numb fingers and for a moment she was speechless, unable to believe that Paul would have concocted such a story. Then it came to her that he was capable of it but . . .

"How did he get the earrings?" she whispered hoarsely. She stared up into Ward's face, willing reality to return and change that ashen mask to the smiling one she had known on her honeymoon. His face wavered and blurred.

"I was hoping you would tell me."

Ward's words beat against her eardrums, his cruel interrogation threatening her sanity. My God, he was as good as accusing her of the theft! She was engulfed in such horror and rage that she scarcely knew what she was saying.

"So you believe your wife is a thief?" she shouted.

"I never said that — I'm just asking for an explanation."

At his words, horror receded and in its place came a fierce anger that gave her strength. "How dare you ask me to defend myself," she hissed. "I never would have suspected you as you do me. No amount of evidence could have made me think you anything less than an honorable man. But that's because . . . because I love you. You wouldn't understand anything about that, of course."

"Calm down — no one has accused you of anything, but you're not exactly acting like an innocent party now, are you?"

Meredith paused for breath, watching him walk to the window where he stopped, his back to her. She marveled that she could have dared to dream that this cold, precise man would come to love her, to really love any woman. The absurdity of such a thing made her bitter and angry all over again.

"Your investigation into my past wasn't as complete as it should have been, Ward. You should have insisted on a more detailed report. You would have found out that during my fifth year at school I stole an eraser, was caught, and had my hands spanked with a ruler. That was the beginning of my criminal career. In junior high school I took a book from a girl's desk, but she missed it, found that I had it, and I had to give it back. Then I got into the big time. I was called to the principal's office because money was missing. Who would have taken it, except the kid who had no money? They were unable to prove that I stole the purse — because I hadn't. But that didn't stop them from talking —"

He swung around and looked at her. "Be quiet, damn you. No one knows about this but you, me, and Crowley. I want to keep it that way."

"You won't tell Francisca and your stepmother? You would deprive them the pleasure of seeing me disgraced?" She threw back the covers and stood up despite the trembling that had set in and threatened to cause her legs to collapse under her. "Oh, how stupid of me. It isn't me you're thinking about. You don't want them to know what a horrible blunder you made when you married me. You married me to spite them, but the joke's on you!" Hysterical laughter burst from her.

He grasped her arms and shook her. "Shut up or I'll slap you."

"You don't slap thieves. You put them in jail. Or do they cut off their hands in Mexico?" Tears were streaming down her face, but she didn't know it.

Ward backed off, his arms held stiffly at his sides. "Stop this nonsense at once!" he barked. "What am I supposed to think? You refuse to tell me a thing about what's really going on between you and that Crowley." The pulse next to his eye was beating furiously.

Meredith returned to the bed and sat down. Her face crumbled, and tears filled her eyes.

"You're obviously in no shape to talk about anything now." Ward sounded disgusted. "Try to get some sleep and I'll see you in the morning."

Meredith couldn't have answered if she tried. Her eyes were screwed tightly shut, her body wracked by dry, silent sobs. When she managed to open her eyes, he was gone.

In all her life she had never felt such crushing anguish. She tried to hate him, but the hate wouldn't come. Sorrow, hurt, and regret came, but not hate. He was suffering, too. There had been sadness in his eyes.

Bitterly she recalled her conversation with Paul. What he had done was so out of character. He zealously guarded his reputation. It wasn't like him to consign something to paper that could be turned against him. How was he to know that Ward wouldn't prosecute? How did he get the earrings? What chance did she have of proving she didn't give the earrings to Paul if he said she did? It didn't really matter — she had known the marriage was doomed for days now. Anyway, she had no intention of allowing herself to be humiliated again in the morning. Her worst fantasy had turned into a living nightmare. She knew she had to get away and now.

Wearily she got up from the bed and began to collect her belongings, stuffing them haphazardly into her suitcase. She took only the things she had brought with her, leaving behind her wedding ring and the gifts and clothes Ward had given her on her honeymoon. She lovingly fingered the shell necklace before placing it on the bureau beside the hammered silver bracelet.

Her packing complete, she dressed in gray slacks and a white cowl-neck sweater. It was useless now to try and impress anyone with her one silk dress that Sophia had pressed so carefully the day she thought it would be her wedding dress.

She wandered for the last time around the beautiful room. She would miss it. And although she had never seen the house in Tulsa, she felt a sense of loss there, too. She would never see it now. Never swim in the pool with Maggie. Maggie! Oh, God, she had forgotten Maggie! The child would think she had deserted her. Her heart ached with the memory of her own desertion, of being left at the county home among strangers. But Maggie would be all right. She had Cullen and Ward.

Ward. It was strange that nothing could alter her feelings for him, not even the fact that he thought her a thief. Would she ever be able to push him back into a small corner of her heart and go on with her life? Would the shame and humiliation she felt at his unspoken accusation ever be dimmed? If he should suddenly open the door and walk in and tell her it was all a mistake, would she be able to forgive and forget? The answer eluded her. Of course it would never happen. Once Ward made up his mind he would not change it easily.

Meredith set her suitcase beside the door and looked at her watch. It was almost three a.m. She slung the strap of her purse over her shoulder and switched off the light. For several minutes she peered out the window. All was quiet. She would leave now. Nothing could induce her to wait until morning and have to walk out of this room past Francisca and Norma. She admitted it was cowardly to slink away, but Ward was convinced of her guilt, so what did it matter if she left the house like a thief in the night.

Without a sound she made her way down the stairs, across the foyer, and out into the courtyard. She was on her way down the drive and still no plan had formed in her mind. She wasn't afraid. What could anyone do to her that was worse than what already had been done? She welcomed the quiet darkness. The sneakers she wore ate up the distance to the first gate. She followed the fence until she found a gap she could squeeze through. She then made her way back to the drive, her feet carrying her on and on.

Later Meredith was to think a guardian angel had sat upon her shoulders. She reached the second gate, crawled through an opening, and followed the ribbon of paving toward Guadalajara. She was beginning to feel the weight of the suitcase when a high-powered car came roaring toward her, its lights making a path in the darkness, blinding her so that she stepped to the side of the road and waited for it to pass. A few yards behind her it screeched to a stop and backed up beside her. A young, girlish voice called to her. "Are you an American?"

"Yes, I am."

"What the devil are you doing out here?" This voice was young and male.

Meredith's mind searched frantically for something to say. "I ran out of gas and I've got to get to the airport."

A tall boy got out of the car. "Come on. We'll take you. Can't have one of our own running around out here this time of the morning. That blond hair stopped us. It would be sure to stop the next car that came along and you might be in trouble."

"Oh, but you were going in the other direction."

"Doesn't matter. Come on. When does your plane leave?" He took her suitcase from her hand and flung it behind the seat. Meredith got in beside the girl. The car lurched ahead, its tires protesting against the paving.

"I really do appreciate this." The corners of Meredith's mouth turned up, obedient to her inner command.

"Where are you from?" The girl was young and pretty in a brittle way.

"Minnesota." Meredith was still holding the smile in place. "And you?"

"Chicago."

"Will your car be okay? It could be stripped by daylight." The young man leaned around the girl to look at Meredith and she wished he would keep his eyes on the road.

"I'll call my friends from the airport and they'll pick it up." She must congratulate herself on lying so magnificently, she thought. She couldn't be here doing these things. She must be insane.

At the airport the boy climbed out and maneuvered her suitcase out from behind the seat, and she took it from his hand.

"I don't know how to thank you. I'd really like to pay you something." She felt like her artificial smile must have set like a plaster cast.

"No. Glad to help out."

"Well, thanks. Thanks a lot. I'd better run. Bye." She walked briskly away.

Luck stayed with her. This was not a popular time of the day to begin a journey, and there was an empty seat on a flight to Brownsville, Texas. They accepted her credit card and she was on her way. Not until then did she allow herself to think about where she was going or what she would do when she got there. She couldn't think now — the hurt and humiliation were too raw.

Chapter Thirteen

It was raining when Meredith arrived in Oklahoma City and the gray skies were in keeping with her mood. It had been a long, tiring trip from Brownsville on the Greyhound bus, but at least she'd had time to think, and there had been no need to use the plastic smile.

She had never been to this part of the country, but she felt drawn to it, maybe because it was near Tulsa — and Ward. For almost two days she wandered around the city looking for accommodations, but it was not until late the second evening that she found an efficiency apartment on Portland Avenue. It was a far cry from the last room she had occupied, but it was clean and cheap.

For the first few days she remained sequestered in her room, too miserable to do more than make a hasty trip to the supermarket down the street and prepare the simplest meal. But by the end of the week the knowledge that her funds were running low forced her out of her shell to face reality.

People didn't die from broken hearts, she told herself. Besides, hers wasn't broken. It was mangled and badly bent, but it was still beating. She had no alternative but to go on living.

After breakfast she put on her sunglasses and walked briskly to the shopping center. April in Oklahoma City was warm, the air scented with budding shrubbery. Newly planted petunias, verbena, carnations, and nasturtiums rested in freshly dug beds. Moss rose lined the walks beneath the mimosa trees. None of this beauty lifted Meredith's spirits.

She had already passed the telephone booths when she decided to call Maude. She turned and retraced her steps. It had been a week since she had left Mexico and in that time she hadn't seen a familiar face or heard a familiar voice. It would be wonderful talking to Jim, too. He always knew how to comfort her. But he was too close to Ward and she didn't dare. She called the operator and paid for three minutes before she heard Maude's voice on the line.

"Hello, Maude?"

"Meredith! Where in the world are you?" Her voice sounded so good, so concerned that it was hard to keep back the tears.

"I've lots to tell you, Maude, but I've only

paid for three minutes. I'll call you another time and fill you in. You'll think you're listening to one of your stories on TV." Meredith fought to control her voice. "How are you? I hope you haven't been worrying about me."

"I've been worried sick about you. Mr. Sanderson called and he wants me to call him if I hear from you."

"No!" She hoped the word hadn't sounded as sharp to Maude's ears as it had to her own. "Don't call him, Maude. Please. I don't want him to know anything about me."

There was a surprised pause on the other end of the line. "I won't tell him if you don't want me to, Meredith. Where are you, child?"

"I'm afraid to tell you now." She shivered. "What did he say?"

"Only that he wanted to get in touch with you. He gave me a number to call if I hear from you."

"Our marriage didn't work out. If he calls again, tell him to have his lawyer prepare the divorce papers and to get in touch with you. I don't want to see him, and I don't want to know anything about him. Someday I'll tell you the whole story, Maude, but not now. Our three minutes are about up, but I'll call you again, soon. Don't worry about me, I'm fine. And Maude . . . I love you." A sob rose in her throat and she hung up the phone.

Too unstrung now to think of looking for a job, Meredith went back to the sanctuary of the apartment. Ward needn't worry, she thought bitterly. She wouldn't ask for a settlement. She wanted to be rid of him as much as he wished to be free of her. Even if he should discover proof of her innocence and want to apologize, it would make no difference. No apology would be able to make up for his earlier doubts. She was too bitter toward him to ever want to see his face again. Bitterness was the only emotion left in her. All others seemed to have been drained away.

Two days later she ventured out again. This time she walked past the row of telephone booths where she had called Maude. A few blocks farther down she passed several fast-food restaurants. Across the street was a small drive-in with a large sign — BILL'S BAR-B-QUE. In the window was a HELP WANTED sign.

Half an hour later Bill gave her the job and handed her the apron. She went to work. It was strictly a takeout order business. She made sandwiches from the meat Bill sliced and placed in the warming trays. The pay was a far cry from what she had received at the hospital, but it was sufficient and she didn't dare seek a job in her field right now because Ward might be trying to trace her. Later, when she'd earned enough money, she would head out to Oregon and take up her profession again. Oregon was beautiful, she knew, and she could start over again there. She walked the six blocks to Bill's and back each day. Some days she went to work as much as an hour early, and if business was good she stayed late to help. She kept every hour of her day occupied and defiantly kept her emotions buried. It was as if she were enclosed in a plastic bubble, aloof and suspended from human contact.

Each day for several weeks she walked past the telephone booths. Gradually the urge to call Maude returned. One evening she yielded to the temptation, called the operator, paid for ten minutes, and asked for Maude's number.

When she heard Maude's voice, she was so glad she had called that it took a while for her to find her own. "This is Meredith. How are you?"

"Land sakes! I could tan your hide. I've been worried sick about you."

"I told you not to worry. I'm fine. I've been busy. I have to walk several blocks to get to the phone and I've just neglected to call." She hated lying to Maude.

"Are you working in a clinic or a hospital? And where are you?"

Meredith answered by asking a question of her own. "Has . . . did you hear anything about the papers I'm to sign?"

"Noooo . . ." The word was drawn out and a suspicion came to Meredith's mind.

"Has Ward called again? Has he been there? Maude, don't believe anything he says about me. Please! You're my only friend and I couldn't bear it if you lost faith in me." The tremor in her voice angered her. Dammit! She'd better not bawl!

"What a thing to say! Nothing could make me lose faith in you. You're like my own child, Meredith. I couldn't love you more if you were my own flesh and blood."

"Thanks for saying that. You've been like a mother to me all these years. I just don't know what I'd do without you."

"Fiddlesticks! When are you coming to see me? You still haven't told me where you are."

"Do you mind if I don't tell you for a while? I'm well and working in a barbeque drive-in. The work is hard, but the food is good." She managed a laugh. "I'll call you again in about a week. If Ward should call, don't tell him anything about me other than that I'll sign whatever he wants me to, and he needn't worry about having to see me."

"Yes, I'll do that, if that's what you want. Don't wait so long to call again."

"I won't. Bye for now."

The next day was her day off. Meredith stayed in all day. She washed her hair, cleaned the room and the kitchenette, did her washing in the bathtub. For the first time in weeks she was able to think rationally. She was wasting her life grieving. She knew she would never love any man again, but that didn't mean she had to remain in a shadow for the rest of her life. One day, perhaps, she would come out into the sunshine and be able to not merely smile with her lips, but with her heart as well. She had always had the resiliency to spring back after she had encountered one of life's unfair blows. She had to make the effort.

The decision was easier to reach than to implement. She had spent so many evenings alone in the room that the habit had become too ingrained to be easily overcome. Like a swimmer taking the plunge into icy water, she decided to walk to the shopping center and see a movie. She threw her trench coat over her arm, because it looked like rain, and left the apartment before she changed her mind. She would see the early show and it would not be too late when she walked home again.

It was with a mixture of unease and increased loneliness that she walked into the darkened theater and found a seat. The movie began and she wished she hadn't come. A beautiful girl walked slowly across the screen to a man, immaculate in dinner jacket. Slowly he came toward her and kissed her mouth, his fingers trembling as he arranged the mink about her shoulders. The girl turned to face him and raised her lips and he gathered her to him and their kiss deepened.

It wasn't until the screen blurred that Meredith realized she was crying. With an angry shake of her head she dug into her pocket for a tissue, berating herself for being such a fool. She'd be glad when the dumb show was over! Next time she would check and see what was playing before she bought her ticket. For the price she paid, she should feel at least as good when she came out as when she went in, she told herself angrily.

It was raining when she came out of the theater. She stood beneath the marquee and put on her trench coat and waited with the other theater patrons for the downpour to slacken. A wind came biting around the corner and she dug her hands into her pockets. Dammit! Why had she chosen this night of all nights to spread her wings? The thought of the warm apartment and a cup of hot cocoa was enough incentive to make her take the first steps out into the rain.

She hurried across the street and gained shelter beneath the canopy that fronted a row of shops. She paused there and pulled the collar of her coat up around her ears. It was then that she saw a man coming across the street. He was walking fast and his limp reminded her of Ward. She turned away. She couldn't bear to look. She didn't want to see anyone or anything that reminded her of Ward.

She bent her head and darted out from beneath the shelter. She shivered and her steps increased. Oh, why hadn't she thought to bring a head-scarf? A gust of wind blew rain in her face, almost blinding her. Something hard grabbed her arm, spinning her around. Frightened, she looked up.

"No!" It couldn't be Ward's tawny eyes staring down at her out of a wet, bleak face! "No!" She said it again.

"Merry." When he spoke she realized he was real and not an apparition.

"Get away from me!" she screamed. "Get away!" Her voice was shrill with the terror that gave her strength to jerk away from him and put her feet into motion. She began to run as if her life depended on it.

Chapter Fourteen

She ran in manic flight along the darkened street, oblivious to the rain, oblivious to the fact that her coat was flying open and she was getting soaked. It didn't enter her mind to wonder how Ward had found her or why he was here. She just wanted to get behind the looked door of her room. She tore across the lawns and through gardens, her shoes leaden with mud.

"What can I do?" she cried out, but she cried into a silence that gave no answer.

She was stripped of everything but fear while groping for the security of a locked room. Her fear was intensified by the path of light that forged out of the darkness. A car was behind her! She darted behind her building and came around to the front and along the walk to her door. It was an eternity before her icy fingers could turn the lock. She slammed the door behind her and threw the dead-bolt in place. Her fingers slowly relaxed their hold on the bolt, and she leaned her head against the door. Her lungs felt as if they were about to burst and her heart thudded as though it had a life of its own. A sharp rap on the door caused her to jerk away from it. The rap came again.

"Let me in, Merry. I want to talk to you."

She held one hand to her aching chest, the other to her mouth while a thousand tiny hammers pounded in her head.

"Open the door, Merry." The voice was louder now, more urgent, and it was followed by several hard raps.

Go away, she screamed silently. If she had a phone she would call the police, she thought wildly.

Bang! He had kicked the door! Had he lost his mind? He'd woken the entire court.

"I'm not leaving until you open the door. I just want to talk to you. What's the matter with you, for God's sake? Open this god-damn door!" The pounding that followed jarred the wall.

"Let him in, lady, or I'll call the police." This was shouted from the apartment opposite hers.

Ward continued pounding on the door.

"Get the hell out of here, fella. Can't you understand she don't want ya?" The shout came from the other end of the court.

"I'm not leaving, Merry. Open the door or there's going to be a big ruckus out here."

All at once she realized the childishness of refusing to let him in. The neighbors might complain to the landlord and she would have to move. Let him in and get it over with, she reasoned with herself even while she was unbolting the door.

He stood there in the pouring rain, almost unrecognizable to her in his sodden condition. She stared, eyes large and frightened. He made no move to come in.

"I have a suitcase in the car. May I bring it in and change into dry clothes?"

She nodded numbly, turned her back on him, and went to the bathroom and began stripping off her own wet things.

When she came out, a kind of brittle calmness possessed her. Ward had turned on the lights and his shoes and dripping wet coat lay near the door. He was kneeling beside an open suitcase and stood with jeans and sweater in his hand. Meredith heard the door to the bathroom close as she opened the folding doors to the tiny kitchenette. She turned the burner on under the tea-kettle and set out two mugs.

In unconscious defiance she had slipped into old jeans and a faded checked shirt. She had toweled her hair and carelessly run the comb through it. Her face was free of make-up. She was pouring the water over the chocolate mix when Ward came up beside her.

"One of these for me? Good! I don't know when I've been so cold."

"I'll sign the papers, Ward. Let's get on with it. I don't want you here." She picked up the hot drink and went to the chair, leaving the couch for him.

He sat down and cupped his hands around the mug. The nerve beside his eye was jumping, but she didn't notice. She knew he was looking at her, but she refused to return his gaze.

"I don't blame you for being bitter, Merry."

"Don't you?"

"I know you didn't take the earrings. I was . . ."

"So? What else is new? I knew that!"

"I realize you must hate the sight of me, but at least let me tell you what happened and give me a chance to apologize."

"If it will make you feel any better, I accept your apology. Now, if you don't mind, I'd like to bow out of your life and get on with mine."

She knew her biting words affected him. His lips tightened and his hand on the cup was shaking.

"That next morning I got to wondering

why Crowley sent me a typed letter. His name was written clearly, too, which is also unusual for a doctor. I went up to Rochester. Needless to say, he was surprised to see me. He was as nervous as a cat on a hot tin roof. He thought I was there to get your check back, which I did, by the way."

He handed her the check. She looked at it and ripped it into several pieces and dropped them on the table.

"Now you know all my little secrets," she said with sardonic emphasis and he looked up sharply.

"Not all, Merry. I don't know what he was threatening you with, but he won't bother you again."

"God must be smiling on me once more."

"I gave Crowley every opportunity to mention returning the earrings. He didn't. If he had, he would have used the occasion to expound on his exemplary character. He's not much of a man." These were the first caustic words he had spoken.

He looked tired, haggard. There were deep creases on each side of his mouth. It hadn't been easy for him, either, Meredith thought, but she refused to soften toward him. He deserved to suffer for what he put her through.

"I don't need you to tell me that, either." Her curt response was openly hostile.

"I went back to Guadalajara and soon discovered who set you up as the thief."

"Francisca." She said it calmly and looked defiantly into his surprised eyes.

"How did you know?"

"She was the only one who hated me enough to do that to me. She was the one who would gain the most if I left. . . ." Her voice cracked and she turned her face away.

"Sophia saw her leaving your room just after you had been there to get your purse. I confronted Francisca and she admitted she took them on an impulse after she heard you talking to Crowley through the double fireplace that connects the library and the sitting room. After she took them she didn't know what to do with them, but Luis did. The scheme was hatched up between them. With you out of the way I'd marry Francisca and their future would be secure. They know my grandmother will not last out the year and that I will want her to be happy."

Meredith's laugh was harsh and hollow. "It sounds more like a soap opera all the time. 'Mistress steals diamonds to frame wife of her lover.' "

His face turned a deep red and their eyes did battle.

"If you meant that to be funny, it isn't." His voice was full of impatience. "I have never been Francisca's lover and wouldn't be if she was the only woman on earth."

"No?" Her cheeks were suffused with color, her balled fist evidence of her anger.

He made an irritated gesture. "I don't understand you. I told you, when I asked you to marry me, that I would be faithful. And we promised we would be honest with each other."

Anger brought her to her feet. "All right, I'll be honest. I want out of the marriage. And just to set the record straight, I overheard you talking to Francisca the night we spent with your grandmother. You said and I quote — 'Meredith will not interfere with *us*, she has nothing to do with *us*, I'll always take care of you . . . nothing has changed between *us*.' Don't sit there and tell me I didn't hear that with my own ears."

His expression mirrored his astonishment. "You took that to mean she is my mistress?"

"I may be naïve, but I'm not stupid!" Her tone implied that he was. "I was going to ask for a divorce even before you practically accused me of being a thief."

He was quiet for so long that she looked at

him and was surprised to see the shadow of pain in his eyes.

"On the strength of what you overheard?" he said in mild reproof.

"Exactly." She looped her hair behind her ears with trembling fingers and walked to the end of the room.

"Part of what you overheard is true," he said to her back. "I didn't think our marriage would change anything between Francisca and me. My responsibility to her is to see that she is taken care of financially. It's my duty." He went to the kitchenette, set his cup on the counter, and returned to the couch.

When Meredith turned to look at him, he was rubbing his thigh and flexing his leg. He looked up to see her watching him and held her eyes with his. Now he could see the ravages in her face, ravages no cosmetics could disguise. Her cheeks were hollow, her skin so pale it seemed to be transparent, and her blue eyes were bruised and sullen.

"Merry." He held out his hand. "Come and sit down and let me tell you about Francisca."

She walked past him and sat down in the chair.

"Francisca's mother was disinherited by my grandmother's father because she married beneath her class. It's a long story, but the gist of it is this. Francisca's mother died and her father married again, and Luis is the result of that marriage."

Meredith shifted uncomfortably. "It isn't necessary for you to tell me your family history."

"I know it isn't," he said evenly, "but I want to." After a pause he continued. "Francisca was only a little child when her mother died. All her life she's felt she's missed out on something because her connection to the family was so weak. For a long time her main goal in life has been to marry me. She saw security and status in being my wife. That's all there is to it. I don't love Francisca. I have never loved her. Often, I don't even like her. I helped her start a business, hoping she would get over her obsession. She's a good businesswoman. As for Luis, I have no blood ties to him, but I've employed him because he is very capable. Needless to say, Luis is no longer on my payroll."

They sat silently, but the tension was alive between them. Meredith's hand shook violently as she raised the cup to her lips and she prayed he wouldn't notice. She felt emotion begin to infiltrate the icy barrier with which she had protected herself. The bitterness she had felt for so long seemed to dissolve in one shuddering sigh, leaving only emptiness.

The lionlike eyes that could seem so fierce looked at her sadly. "I can't tell you how sorry I am for coming to you before I found out the truth. But even though I behaved badly, you should never have run away — you should have weathered the storm."

She stared at him with eyes dilated with pain.

"It's impossible for me to forget you doubted me. Regardless of what evidence anyone had given me about you, it wouldn't have shaken my faith. I'd never have believed you a thief." Her lower lip quivered.

"Perhaps not, but you did believe that I was unfaithful to you, and surely that's much worse. The truth is, Meredith, that you doubted me as much as I doubted you."

She realized that what he said was true. If she hadn't already believed that Ward didn't — couldn't — love her, she never would have left.

"When we're hurt and angry," Ward continued, "we all say things we don't mean. I was angry and I was hurt and disappointed. I thought you wanted Crowley. Most of all I was angry at myself for allowing my feelings to get so involved with a woman."

He stood up. She knew he was looking at the top of her head. "I want to be honest with you, Merry. I never believed I'd truly love someone. Any ideals I ever cherished were smashed at a very early age. All the women I met seemed the same. They wanted a man to desire them and they set out to provoke physical desire. Then their mercenary little heads took over." He stood there and seemed to be waiting for her to look up or say something. "When I met you I knew you were different." He said it softly and she felt his hand lightly touch her hair. "I knew you would be faithful to me, but even before we were married I wanted more. I wanted your love as well."

She looked up, now, at his unsmiling mouth and with all her heart she wanted to believe him. But conviction refused to come. She got up quickly. She had to move away from him so she could think. She went to the sink and rinsed her cup. When she turned he was beside her.

"I keep thinking about what you said that night. You said you would have believed me because you loved me."

"One will say most anything when one's desperate." She tried to laugh, but her eyes were frightened, like those of a trapped animal.

He grabbed her forearms and jerked her toward him. "I can't lose you!" His eyes glinted like amber agates and the strength of his fingers brought a bruising, physical pain. "We had the beginning of something good. Better than good — wonderful! Like the gold at the end of the rainbow."

Her voice choked on a cry and her face crumbled helplessly. Great tearing sobs shook her, and with a soft groan he pulled her against his chest.

"Don't cry, darling. Don't cry," he said against the top of her head. He held her close, waiting for the storm of tears to spend itself. "Hurry, darling," she heard him say. "Hurry and stop crying so I can kiss you." Firm fingers raised her chin and a soft handkerchief wiped her eyes and nose, then his lips were on hers.

She felt the warmth of his breath before she felt the heat of his mouth as it parted hers, his arms drawing her to him. Yielding, her arms went around him and he pulled her even closer.

"I love you," he whispered against her lips. "God, how I love you! I've been through hell these past few weeks. I could have killed Francisca and Luis!"

She was trembling and wildly flushed. A corner of her mind still couldn't believe he could love her. She put her hand on his chest and held herself away from him.

"Please . . . don't say something you don't mean. I couldn't bear it."

He looked at her with half-closed eyes, a passionate satisfaction on his face.

"Before God, I love you. I want you for the rest of my life. You *are* my life! I was so wrong about love, darling. It is real. It's both hurtful and wonderful!" Her heart turned over. She closed her eyes and leaned her forehead against his shoulder. "Put your arms around me, darling." There was an anguish in his voice that pierced her like a thorn. "Hold me. Tell me you love me. I need assurance, too."

"I do love you." Her arms went tight around him. "I thought I was going to die from it, I love you so much."

They stood locked together in the middle of the room. Their embrace was like finally coming home, like finding a safe harbor in a storm, truly like reaching the pot at the end of the rainbow.

The rain continued all night. The wind came up and tortured the trees, and lightning flashed, making an eerie light in the darkened room. Ward and Meredith lay in the pull-down bed oblivious to everything but each other. They talked in snatches of whispers between kisses.

"Are you sure this thing won't fold up in the wall like they do in the movies?"

"I'm not sure of anything right now." She laughed happily.

"No? Not even one thing?"

"Well . . . it's still raining," she teased, hovering over him.

He crushed her down to him and rolled over, pinning her softness beneath him.

"I'm aching for you and you tease me!" He ran his hands down her slim body. He framed her chin with his hand. She felt the faint tremor in his fingers, felt the quickening of his breathing. "I couldn't bear to lose you again," he whispered hoarsely. "You make me come alive!"

"Please . . ." she whispered, and a hunger like an intense, physical pain pierced her. She clung to him desperately, her body young and alive.

"Sweetheart, my love . . ." He whispered love words softly and his mouth traveled over her face to meet her lips again and again, hard and demanding at first, then tenderly, as his tongue moved to part her lips and explore the sweetness of her mouth. Her fingers loved every part of him and she moved slowly and lovingly over him. It had been so long since she had held him, and even then it wasn't like this.

He seemed to read her thoughts. "Loving makes all the difference," he murmured.

Afterward they lay amid the rumpled sheets feeling weak and satisfied, engulfed by a warm, sweet lethargy. Her arms were around his neck, her limbs molded to his, and his tender caresses felt like the calm after a storm.

"How did you find me?" It was the first time she had thought about it.

His eyes shone like bright stars and his lips twitched.

"I don't know if I should tell you. You might turn me over to the police." He kissed her soundly. "I put a tracer on Maude's telephone. It's against the law, but I was desperate. I traced the booth where you made the call and found the drive-in where you worked. All I had to do was patrol the neighborhood until I found you. I saw you come out of the theater and got out of the car to come meet you. I didn't dream you would run from me. Don't do that again, my love — ever."

"Did Maude know you tapped her telephone?"

"No. She was as protective of you as a

mother goose. She called me a dumb coot for letting you get away from me. Do you approve of people calling your husband a dumb coot?"

"Maude said that?" Laughter bubbled up.

"And more. She's fiercely devoted to you. I'm glad she's a she."

"You're nuts! Do you know that?"

He kissed her long and hard while running his hands down her slender form. In the middle of the bed they lay entwined, content to be there close together. Meredith wound her arms around her husband's neck and pressed herself closer to him. This was home. The safest, most wonderful place in all the world. This long, lean body pressed to hers was the torch that lighted her life.

"Are you going with me on my honeymoon?" he asked in a voice stripped of all seriousness.

"Sure, if Bill will give me a few days off."

"I might have to punch Bill in the nose."

"On second thought, maybe the barbecue industry can survive without me."

"It's going to have to, because I can't," he said huskily and began to make beautiful, tender love to her.

The employees of Thorndike Press hope you have enjoyed this Large Print book. All our Thorndike and Wheeler Large Print titles are designed for easy reading, and all our books are made to last. Other Thorndike Press Large Print books are available at your library, through selected bookstores, or directly from us.

For information about titles, please call:

(800) 223-1244

or visit our Web site at:

www.gale.com/thorndike
www.gale.com/wheeler

To share your comments, please write:

Publisher
Thorndike Press
295 Kennedy Memorial Drive
Waterville, ME 04901